The dazzling blue e[illegible] held a glint of amusement. [illegible] and *you* picked yourself up and bounc[illegible] [illegible]ain.'

Charlotte's mouth d[illegible]pped open. She flashed him a startled look and blushed. 'Sorry?'

'We have met before, you know. St Chad's—night duty?'

'Oh, so you did remember me.' She laughed self-conciously. 'I-I was hoping you hadn't.'

'Were you? Why?'

Charlotte wrinkled her nose. 'We-ell, you must have thought I was a drip that night. I mean, I was really pathetic—something I would rather forget about. And there was I thinking you were miles away. Didn't it work out for you in Canada?'

'Oh, that. I was only making a private visit, not taking up residence. As a matter of fact, I found your bounce-back attitude thought-provoking. Which was why I remembered you,' he explained.

Finding herself the focus of his steady gaze was disconcerting . . .

Grace Read has had a life-long love affair with nursing. Starting as a Red Cross Nurse in a London hospital during the war, she went on to do her general training in the Midlands. Marriage and a baby ended that career, but she retains a keen interest in the profession. She has a son and two daughters. Her youngest daughter is a nursing sister and keeps 'Mum' abreast of modern trends, vetting her novels for medical accuracy. When she is not writing Grace enjoys gardening, travelling to research backgrounds, and admits to a fondness for golden Labradors.

Tides of the Heart is her tenth Doctor Nurse Romance; previous titles include *Nurse in a Quandary, Call Dr Knight*, and *Casualties of Love.*

TIDES OF THE HEART

BY

GRACE READ

MILLS & BOON LIMITED
ETON HOUSE 18-24 PARADISE ROAD
RICHMOND SURREY TW9 1SR

First published in Great Britain 1988
by Mills & Boon Limited

This edition 1988

ISBN 0 263 76151 7

Set in Baskerville 11 on 11½ pt.
03 – 0888 – 53538

Typeset in Great Britain by JCL Graphics, Bristol

Made and printed in Great Britain

CHAPTER ONE

CHARLOTTE Blythe carried her weekend bag down the crooked staircase, left it in the oak-beamed hallway and wandered into the large, flagged farmhouse kitchen. Mrs Woods, her father's daily help, glanced up from her task of bottle-feeding a newly-born lamb.

'Oh, will you not be stopping for some tea, my love?' she asked, her plump cheeks creasing into a smile. 'I'll be finished here in a minute.'

'No, it's all right, Woody, I have to get back.' Charlotte idly scratched the head of the little woolly creature tugging away at its bottle. 'There's a retirement party for one of the senior partners at the practice, and she's a really nice person, so I'd like to be there.'

Mrs Woods eyed with affection the slender girl, clad in jeans and a colourful sweater, whom she had seen grow from a timid leggy teenager with corn-coloured hair tied in bunches, to the independent and attractive young woman she now was. It was amazing the difference a few years could make.

'Well now, don't you worry about your old dad. We're managing fine. He's a real proud of you, you know,' she added with a nod of her greying head.

Perching on a corner of the scrubbed table—something she would have thought twice about if her Aunt Hannah had still been in charge—Charlotte responded with a wry grin. 'He'd have been better pleased if I'd been a boy, gone to agricultural college and come back to help on the farm.'

'Don't you believe it, lass. He's a man of few words, is your dad, but deep down he thinks the world of you, and he's come out of himself a lot since your aunt left.'

'I suppose he's bound to miss her after all these years,' Charlotte mused.

Mrs Woods tipped up the bottle as the lamb drained the last of its feed. 'A good miss, I'd say,' she remarked drily.

'Well, I don't deny that things are a little more relaxed around here since she's been gone,' Charlotte agreed with a quiet smile.

Her father himself came in from the yard just then, bringing with him a breath of the great outdoors. A man of average height, lean but well-muscled and with a healthy complexion, John Blythe flung his flat tweed cap on a peg behind the door and smoothed his thick brown hair with both hands. 'Oh, you're off now, are you?' He gave his daughter a casual but discerning glance. She grew more like her mother every time he saw her. Not that he'd seen too much of her over the past few years since she had made London her stamping ground.

'Yes, Dad. It's been a lovely weekend. Now that I'm nearer I must try to get home more often.' What she didn't say was now that her Aunt Hannah had left, coming home would be a pleasure and not a penance.

One of Charlotte's abiding childhood memories was of being hauled to the bottom of the garden by her mother's sister, and soundly slapped. Her crime, daring to slip into the bedroom to see her mother who was desperately ill. She had died on Charlotte's seventh birthday, since which time Hannah had run the Blythe household to her own satisfaction if not to theirs.

A few months ago, however, Hannah had surprised everyone by marrying a retired Army major and going off to help him run his country pub. And the difference in the atmosphere at Coppice Farm was unbelievable. After the first shock, her departure had brought a sense of relief all round, and Charlotte was aware of a subtle change in her father's manner. He was like a man released from bondage.

'So you think you'll settle in this new job, do you?' he asked, draping his padded weatherproof jacket beneath the cap and going to the sink to wash his hands. 'Doesn't it seem tame being a dogsbody in a country practice after your grand London hospital?'

'Do you mind?' Charlotte said with mock indignation. 'I'm not a dogsbody. I'm a very important part of the set-up. And there's lots of interesting things going on in this part of the world. Anyway, I got this urge for the wide open spaces. Back to my roots!' she dramatised.

Her father gave her a crooked smile, consulted his wristwatch and went to the dresser to alter the hands of the old French ormolu clock standing there. 'It's been a love-hate relationship with me these last few months.' He stood back to admire his newly-acquired treasure. 'Perhaps I ought to sell up and go into antiques.'

'Oh, come on,' teased Charlotte, 'who are you kidding? You'd be lost without the farm.'

Mrs Woods shook her head indulgently. 'Aye, it's been a cruel spring and I daresay it won't be the last, but I reckon you'd be like a fish out o' water in any place else.' She put the orphan lamb in a box by the Aga and followed father and daughter out to where Charlotte's blue Metro waited in front of the York stone farmhouse.

John Blythe offered his cheek as Charlotte turned to kiss him goodbye. 'Mind how you go now,' he said a trifle gruffly, patted her on the shoulder and closed the car door after her.

'OK . . . I'll phone you some time.' She gave a cheery wave and drove off down the farm lane towards the country road that would take her back to Niddborough. But the smile on her face hid the ache in her heart, the longing for some show of real warmth from her father. He was a quiet, self-contained man who found it difficult to express affection. This weekend though, maybe with her aunt's influence no longer at work, Charlotte felt that they had come a little closer, which was encouraging.

It was a good twenty miles from the Vale of York to the thriving ancient market town where Charlotte now lived. She had recently started a new career there as a group practice nurse at the purpose-built health centre where three local doctors had their consulting rooms. And the job was proving to be very much to her liking so far, with its regular hours and weekends off.

Driving through the peaceful countryside on this quiet Sunday evening, she was glad to be back among the rolling fells where the passing seasons annually staged the survival of the life force. Sturdy drystone walls chequered the landscape, lapwings and curlews wheeled and soared in carefree flight, and sheep cropped tranquilly as they had done for centuries.

Even in late April there was still snow on the distant moortops, but down in the fertile valleys the roadsides were alight with daffodils and cottage gardens were beginning to burgeon. This land of ancient castles, tumbling rivers, soaring heights and secluded hamlets, its beauty was awe-inspiring. Despite earlier, unhappy memories, Charlotte felt a lift to her heart as the verdant acres sped by.

As she skirted a village green with its cluster of grey stone dwellings, a wayside pulpit in the ancient churchyard caught her attention. It proclaimed . . .

The tide never goes out so far
but it always comes in again.

She reflected on that, turning it over in her mind. Yes, it was true; life ebbed and flowed between the good times and the bad and all you had to do in the bad times was to hang on until things got better. A year ago she had thought she would never get over Phil—her world had seemed in ruins. Now here she was with a challenging new job and the past resolutely left behind her in the teeming streets of London.

At first the informality of the small provincial

health centre had seemed strange after the strict regime of the great London teaching hospital, but she had soon adapted to the change and the closer ties with patients. It brought more personal responsibility but more satisfaction as well. Neither could she have wished for nicer living arrangements than sharing a house with Lynne, who was the local district nurse. They had been kindred spirits right from the start and had become good friends over the three months they had been together.

So, on the face of it, everything should now be rosy. And would have been, but for that chance sighting in the High Street when she had been setting off for her weekend home. Thinking back, Charlotte sighed heavily.

She had called in at the nearby general stores to buy chocolates for Mrs Woods and some whisky for her father. As she entered the cluttered shop her eyes were drawn to the post-office counter where a tall, dark-haired man in a thick Arran sweater was buying stamps. As she caught a sideways glimpse of his square-jawed profile, a quiver slid down her spine. It *was* him, wasn't it? Whatever was he doing here in a small Yorkshire town in the Dales? She didn't suppose for one moment that he would remember her, but just in case, she stayed out of sight behind the magazine rack until he left the shop.

For much of the weekend the incident had haunted her and the memory of their previous brief encounter had come vividly to mind. In the early hours of the morning it was. She had been at St Chad's then, night duty on Men's Medical, and with an agitated cardiac patient complaining of chest pains she had been obliged to bleep the medical registrar.

The doctor who answered her call was not one of the familiar young medics who usually arrived, weary-eyed in crumpled white coat. This was a more mature man, completely self-assured, dark hair slightly rumpled, but deep blue eyes wide awake. 'What's the problem, Nurse?' he had asked in a voice that resounded pleasantly in her ears.

Confronted by this stranger, she was somewhat taken aback. 'Oh! Are you new here?' she returned, doubtfully.

He met her wary gaze with a slight smile. 'Sort of new/old. I'm a product of this med school, but long before your time, I expect. Night Sister will vouch for me. The name's Bob Challoner, and I'm acting locum for tonight. OK?'

Charlotte felt herself go pink, but there had been a hue and cry at the time over a bogus character who had fooled everybody. 'Sorry,' she said, 'only we've been told to be careful.'

'Yes, I know. Now, what can I do for you?'

'It's Mr Chambers . . .' She explained about the patient, a middle-aged man who had been transferred from the coronary care unit the previous day. 'He's feeling anxious about being back in the general ward. It may be just the usual reaction after being fussed over in CCU. His monitor seems OK, but I thought I ought to make sure.'

Dr Challoner nodded and walked with her to the bedside, but upon examination he could find no obvious cause for alarm. After reassurance and some Diazepam to allay his fears, Mr Chambers settled down to sleep.

'Don't hesitate to call me back if you're at all worried,' the doctor had said upon leaving.

Once more peace reigned as the darkened ward settled down to its normal sleeping pattern. Somnolent breathing and the occasional snore were all that disturbed the silence.

Having sent the student nurse for her meal break, Charlotte quietly made a routine check on the rest of the patients before sitting down in the shaded light of the office desk. She leafed through the Kardex to remind herself of a few special procedures to be carried out in the morning. Then she changed a transfusion bag and recorded a sleeping pulse before making herself coffee to stave off the three a.m. drowsiness which threatened.

As she waited for her drink to cool, her thoughts turned inward for a moment to this latest disaster in her life. Phil's deception had shocked and shattered her. There's a fool born every minute, and that's me! she thought dejectedly. Well, never again. She would be much more cautious in future. What was so great about marriage anyway? It wasn't the be-all and end-all for women these days.

Footfalls and the flap of the ward doors shook her out of her black moment and she glance up to see Dr Challoner returning.

'I was just across the way and I thought I'd look in to see that you were all right,' he said.

'Yes, fine. Everything's quiet.' She raised a smile. 'Would you like a coffee?'

He nodded, his dark-lashed eyes creasing at the corners. 'That would be very welcome. I'll just check on your Mr Chambers . . .'

Charlotte made the drink and presently he joined her in the office, sitting in a comfortable easy chair, long legs stretched out in front of him. 'He's fine. No other problems?' he queried, eyebrows raised.

'No . . .' she half-laughed, 'at least, nothing that you can do anything about.'

'Ah! I thought you looked rather fed up. What's wrong?'

Charlotte didn't honestly know what had made her say that, but having done so she felt an explanation seemed to be called for. She hesitated for a moment, then said lightly, 'Oh, just the old eternal triangle. He was married.'

A dimple flickered in Robert Challoner's lean cheek. 'So you got your little fingers burned, eh? That'll learn you!'

'Thanks a bunch. Actually I didn't know he was *still* married. He'd told me he was divorced, but he was only separated. I went to his flat unexpectedly one night, and found his wife there. And she was pregnant. And threatening to commit suicide if he didn't go back to her. It was awful.' She chewed her lip, remembering.

'Oh dear. I'm sorry.' His eyes and his voice were sympathetic. 'I apologise for the whole of my backsliding sex. Try not to let it spoil your faith in human nature.'

'Oh, I shall bounce back. I usually do.'

'Usually do? That sounds as of you've had a whole string disasters.'

Charlotte smiled. 'Not all in *that* category, thank goodness, but my life has been a bit fraught here and there.'

He waited, his studied gaze inviting confidence and, unpredictably, she found herself baring her soul, telling him things she had never put into words before. There was her despair when her older, much-loved brother had a fatal brain haemorrhage. There was the added trauma of her mother's death soon after giving birth to a stillborn boy.

'My mother's sister came to keep house for us then, and she wasn't an easy person to get on with. Besides which, I grew up with a sense of guilt for being alive,' Charlotte confessed. 'I overheard her say it was a pity it was the boys who were taken, and I assumed my father felt the sam. Which was why I came into nursing originally—to get away. I needed to justify my existence. Really, though, Aunt Hannah did me a favour,' she mused, 'because I like my job and I can't imagine doing anything else.'

'Bereavement makes people say and do unaccountable things,' the doctor reflected, 'and adults don't always realise how sensitive children can be. That chance remark you overheard, they'd probably be shocked to know you took it personally. You don't still feel guilty, do you?'

'No, what the heck! I'm a girl and I can't change that. Anyway, I should have made an awful boy. I certainly wouldn't have made a livestock farmer. I cry at the drop of a hat. I nearly died when my pet lamb had to go.'

He grinned and looked her over approvingly. 'There's not much wrong with your image that I can see. We're all cowards at heart. And I daresay you're a lot tougher than you know. You have to be, or you wouldn't last long in this game.'

'So what brought you into medicine?' she prompted, beginning to feel self-conscious at having talked so much about herself.

'Mmm . . .that's something I keep asking myself. Let's say it seemed like a good idea at the time. I started out in computers, then I decided that the human condition was far more interesting than technology.'

She wondered if there might have been more to it than that, but the student nurse coming back from her meal brought their confidences to an end.

Robert Challoner rose to leave 'Well, I probably shan't see you again,' he told her. 'This is my last night here, and then I'm off to Canada. All the best, though. It's been nice meeting you. I enjoyed our little chat.'

The following morning Charlotte has been filled with misgivings at having bared her soul to a stranger. She didn't know what on earth could have possessed her, except that in the small hours, on a darkened ward, one's defences fell away. Oddly, there had seemed to be a kind of affinity between them out of all proportion to the situation which had brought them together. She had comforted herself with the knowledge that she was unlikely ever to see him again. And that was the last she *had* seen of him until three days ago.

Now, on reaching the town, Charlotte passed the small general stores where she had seen him again, and the whole episode sprang vividly to mind. She could recall the entire conversation as if it were yesterday. Like a brilliantly-lit stage set the scene came into focus and the memory of it brought her out in a sweat. Perhaps he had just been passing through, she thought hopefully. There had been an international medical conference in Leeds the previous week which might account for his presence in this part of the world.

It was seven o'clock by the time Charlotte reached the outskirts of the town. The modest grey stone terraced house she shared with Lynne was one of a row of similar houses in Spinney Lane, a grass-verged side-street. Putting her key in the lock, she let herself into the small space which served for their hall. There were stairs leading up to the bedrooms and an open archway which gave access to the living-room.

The sound of pop music drifted down to her as she peeled off her warm jacket and hung it on a peg.

'Hi, Lynne, I'm back!' she called up. 'I'm making a coffee . . . want some?'

'Please . . . won't be a jiff,' Lynne sang out.

Making her way to the kitchen, Charlotte got busy, and presently her friend came skipping down to join her. Lynne's curvy figure was draped in a blue towelling bathrobe, her curly brown hair bunched on top of her head with a ribbon. She reached for the biscuit tin. 'I'm starving . . . an apple and a banana is all I've had all day. Thought I'd better save myself for tonight.'

'How's the weight going?' Charlotte asked brightly, reaching for the mugs and spooning the coffee granules.

'Abysmally!' Lynne sighed, perching on the step-stool and nibbling. 'I went to Weight Watchers on Friday and I'd put *on* two pounds.' Her round face was mournful. 'Honestly, I've been ever so good.

Even refused a bit of Mrs Marlowe's iced gingerbread. My tummy's constantly on the rumble.'

'Oh dear!' Charlotte laughed sympathetically. 'Never mind. Curves are coming back into fashion, they say.'

'Oh well, perhaps I'll settle for being fashionable then.' Lynne dropped a sweetener into her drink and stirred. 'Did you have a nice weekend?'

'Mmm . . . not bad.' Levering herself on to the top of the working surface, Charlotte cupped her mug in her hands. 'Decided I ought to encourage my dad to get our more, so I took him to Ripon where they were doing *Die Fledermaus*. It was jolly good.' She paused and then went on, 'D'you know, when I first got home I found myself tidying up and putting everything straight the way Aunt Hannah used to. Then I thought, blow this! So I left the newspapers on the coffee table, and Dad's slippers under the sideboard, and I put the cushions in different chairs, and I threw out the artificial flowers and picked some daffs from the garden. Hannah wouldn't have real flowers in the house, she said they made too much mess.'

Lynne chuckled. 'Come the revolution! I wonder if her new husband knows what he's in for?'

'He's nice, actually,' Charlotte admitted, 'I liked him. A strong-minded character though, I don't think he'll stand for being bossed around.'

'Perhaps that's what she needed all along, a masterful mate.'

'Yes, maybe. They'll probably be good for each other. My dad's bound to miss her for a time, but he's got Mrs Woods. She's been with us for years, and she doesn't object to his clocks ticking all over the place.'

Lynne frowned. 'Clocks?' she said.

'Yes, my dad's a clock fanatic. He picks them up at auctions and junk shops. He just enjoys taking them apart and putting them in good working order. Used to drive Hannah mad when they all started chiming,' Charlotte chuckled. 'So, what's new here?' she went on.

'Doctor Mac's wife had her baby yesterday. He's over the moon. It's a little boy.'

'Oh, great! She all right?'

'Yes, she had a Caesarean section so she won't be home for a while.'

As yet Charlotte hadn't attended a social occasion with her new collegues. 'What kind of gear do we wear tonight?' she asked.

'Anything, really. It won't be formal. Doctor Marion doesn't stand on ceremony.'

'No, she's lovely, isn't she? I'm really sorry she's going. I wonder who we'll get in her place? Have you heard?'

'No, but it'll probably be a bloke because Wendy Fenner took the place of Doctor Barr when he retired. What do you think of Wendy?' Lynne asked.

Charlotte pursed her lips and looked thoughtful. 'We-el, I haven't had a great deal to do with her so far. Not personally, I mean. She seems OK as regards work, and she's got everything going for her, hasn't she? Brains and good looks.'

'Yeah, I wouldn't mind her figure,' Lynne

sighed. She glanced up at the Willow-Pattern kitchen wall clock. 'Hey, we'd better get a move on or all the food will be gone.'

'Right!' Charlotte finished her coffee, slipped off her perch and ran upstairs to wash and change. Searching through her wardrobe, she chose a sea-green jersey silk dress which was easy to wear, uncrushable, and moulded becomingly to her slender figure. She flicked a brush through her soft fair hair which fell easily into its swinging casual style. Next, she carefully applied some light eye make-up, blusher and lip-gloss, fastened on a pair of chunky gold earrings, and was ready for her first real party since leaving London.

Lynne had teamed a flattering straight black skirt with a red silk shirt.

'You look terrific,' Charlotte told her admiringly. 'Honestly, I don't know why you worry about your figure.'

Her friend wrinkled her nose. 'It's all very well for you to talk, Lotty.' She smoothed her hips. 'Seriously, this does make me look slimmer, doesn't it?'

Charlotte agreed that it did. 'Who are you hoping to impress?' she asked mildly. 'Anyone I know?'

'No, no one in particular. *Be Prepared,* that's my motto. I wasn't a Girl Guide for nothing. Come on, let's go. Whose car shall we take—yours or mine?'

'Oh, we'll take mine . . .then if someone interesting shows up you'll be a free agent,' Charlotte added, her lively green eyes twinkling. She had come to realise that Lynne was for ever on the lookout for Mr Right.

They set off in carefree mood for the half-hour drive to the country hotel where the party was being held. Friars Court was a seventeenth-century mansion situated high on the edge of the moors and set in its own attractive parkland. Night had fallen and the sky was heavy with banking cloud as they drew up on the forecourt of the floodlit grey stone building, a bright oasis against the backcloth of brooding heights.

With cheeks glowing from the nip in the air, the girls hurried into the welcoming warmth of the richly-carpeted foyer. Public rooms were on the ground floor but private functions were held in an upstairs room. Climbing the graceful, curving staircase, they left their coats in the cloakroom before seeking out their hosts from among the friendly crowd already assembled.

Dr Marion Bates was a pleasant, comfortably-built woman in her late sixties. She greeted the nurses warmly and introduced her husband. 'Ben, you've met Lynne before, haven't you? And this is Charlotte, she's our practice nurse. Hasn't been with us long, but she's already indispensable. I believe the patients often ask to see her instead of the doctor!'

Charlotte laughed. 'That's only because they think I'm easier to get hold of without an appointment. *I didn't like to bother the doctor,*' she clowned, to general laughter.

'I only wish I'd had the support of a good nurse in my early days,' Dr Marion remarked. 'The rest of the partners will be quite spoiled. I am going to miss you all,' she sighed, 'but better to go before I'm old and doddery.'

'And perhaps *I* can have a bit more of your attention in my declining years,' put in her husband benignly.

After a lighthearted discussion about their retirement plans and with good wishes expressed, the girls move on to make way for other guests arriving.

A tempting buffet was set out on a long table at one side of the room, while at another table the sandy-bearded Dr Gordon McAllister—or Mac as he was popularly known—was making himself useful pouring drinks.

'Hallo! We hear congratulations are in order,' Lynne breezed when they gravitated over towards the refreshments.

Dr Mac, radiating goodwill to all, withdrew the cork from another bottle of wine. 'Yes. Me a dad! I can hardly believe it.'

'You soon will,' said Charlotte with a smile, taking the drink he handed her. 'Well, here's to baby Mac,' she went on, raising her glass to him. 'Was it a boy you both wanted, or didn't you mind?'

'Naomi wasn't fussed, but if I'm honest I'm quite chuffed it's a boy. A chap likes to have a son, doesn't he?'

Lynne helped herself to a smoked salmon finger. 'Some chaps say *Thank Heaven for Little Girls!*'

'True,' returned Mac with a rakish grin. 'Where should we be without 'em—if only to produce the little boys!' He dodged out of harm's way as both girls threatened to tip their drinks over him.

The conversation took on a more serious note as

they enquired after the well-being of his wife and the important details concerning the baby.

'I imagine our social life will go to pot for a wee while,' the new father said with a fond sigh, 'although Naomi's determined not to let him rule our lives.'

'Well, if ever you need a baby-sitter, just let me know,' Charlotte offered.

'Mmm . . . that goes for me, too.' Lynne's eyes flickered across the room and sparked with interest, focussing on the couple being greeted by their hosts. 'Who's that with Dr Fenner?' she asked. 'Boyfriend?'

Mac glanced over at the pair in question. 'Oh no, that's Marion's replacement, Robert Challoner.'

Charlotte also had turned to look—and her heart began to thump. *Oh no!* she thought. But the new partner was indeed the man she had seen in the post office, the stranger she had opened her heart to in the middle of the night all those months ago. Elegantly clad in grey lounge suit and deep blue shirt, thick dark hair brushed back from his broad forehead, Robert Challoner caused quite a few heads to turn in his direction.

'You've not met him yet girls?' Mac went on cheerfully. 'Well, they're coming this way. Stick around and I'll introduce you.'

CHAPTER TWO

AS THE couple drew nearer, Charlotte felt her cheeks burn and she swallowed nervously. Robert Challoner probably wouldn't remember her anyway, she tried to reassure herself. After all, she must have been a fairly anonymous figure at the time. One staff nurse must look much like another in a darkened ward in the small hours of the morning. He'd probably met hundreds of other nurses since then, and if he didn't recognise her, she was certainly not going to remind him.

It failed to strike her that a lissom, fair-haired girl sitting in a pool of light from the green-shaded lowered lamp was far from forgettable. However, when introductions were made Dr Challoner showed no obvious signs of having met her before, and she breathed more easily.

As always, Dr Wendy Fenner looked poised and exquisite. Tall and slim, with her shoulder-length dark hair expertly styled, tonight in her cream dress she looked the last word in chic simplicity. Beside her Charlotte felt like a country mouse.

'Wendy . . .how are you?' Dr Mac kissed her lightly on the cheek. 'Good evening, Robert.' He shook hands with the new partner and went on, 'This is Lynne, she's one of our district nurses, and this is Charlotte, our practice nurse.'

Robert Challoner shook hands formally with them both and they exchanged polite greetings.

'You'll find Charlotte a tremendous help,' Wendy volunteered brightly, 'she relieves us of all those tiresome chores like cervical screening, and inoculations, and the MOTs.'

'MOTs?' The new GP raised a dark eyebrow in Charlotte's direction.

She laughed softly, more relaxed now that she saw no trace of recognition in his deep blue eyes. 'That's what we call the routine health checks we've just started to do.'

'Where were you before coming here, Robert?' Lynne enquired.

'In Leeds actually, doing paediatrics at the Infirmary. I'm looking forward to being at the grass roots end of things. Perhaps life will be a little less hectic than of late.'

'You'll be lucky!' scoffed Mac.

'Have you found somewhere nice to live?' Charlotte asked, feeling she should add something to the conversation.

'Well, I'm in rented accommodation for the time being, but I shall look for something to buy later. Then I'll need some feminine advice on the matter of decor.' His mouth puckered humorously. 'Any offers?'

Wendy flashed him a beguiling smile. 'When you've found something I'm sure you won't be short of good advice, Rob, from a great many quarters.'

She already seemed to be on familiar terms with the new partner and presently took him off to talk with Professor Frith, the surgical consultant.

Lynne gazed after them. 'They seem to be getting on rather well,' she mused. 'Did they know each other before this?'

Mac said he wasn't aware of it, but that it looked as if they might soon be knowing each rather better. 'Watch this space!' he joked.

Compared with the fairly riotous parties which took place at St Chad's Hospital when Charlotte was there, tonight's affair was quite low key. She and Lynne were among the younger minority, nevertheless it was an agreeable crowd, and as the evening progressed she warmed to her new circle of friends. Amongst others there were the practice receptionists and their partners, and Ruth, their kindly health visitor, and curly-haired Bryan Dalgleish from the local pharmacy. There was also staff from the Valley Community Hospital which was mainly serviced by the GPs and consultants.

Charlotte had no further contact during the evening with Robert Challoner, but inevitably her gaze was drawn often in his direction. Being, as she thought, unrecognised had taken a weight off her mind, and she observed him with more detachment. He would make a good family doctor, she decided. The determined set of his jaw suggested a man who knew what he was about, but there was good humour in his expression, which would put patients at their ease. From experience she knew he was also a good listener, a desirable trait for a general practitioner. There was certainly no reason why she should not develop the same good working relationship with him that she enjoyed with the other two partners.

The evening came to an end about eleven p.m. after a tribute had been paid to the retiring partner by Professor Frith. Then everyone sang 'For she's a jolly good fellow', and the party broke up amid a general feeling of bonhomie.

Having collected their coats, Charlotte and Lynne began making their way down to the foyer, still chatting animatedly to each other on the stairs.

'Not the most exciting night out I've ever had, but it wasn't bad, was it?' Lynne said.

'No, I really enjoyed it, and I got to know a few more people. I thought that anaesthetist from the hospital, Ken Jameson, rather fancied you. Pity he got called away,' remarked Charlotte with a smile.

'Mmm, but all is not lost! He's promised to show me an old Army surgical kit which his great grandfather used in the Crimean . . .' As Lynne spoke her foot slipped, she lost a shoe and pitched headlong down the last half-dozen stairs.

'Lynne!' Charlotte picked up the shoe and hurried to where her friend lay sprawling. 'Are you hurt?'

Sitting up and nursing her right arm, Lynne bit back the tears. 'I-I think I've . . . done in my wrist . . .'

Other people gathered around and she was helped to a chair.

'Any bones broken?' The deep voice came from Robert Challoner who had been following them down.

'It's her wrist,' Charlotte explained in an anxious tone.

'Let me see.' He squatted down in front of Lynne to examine the rapidly swelling and misshapen joint.

Wendy Fenner, a sable jacket over her cream dress, had by now also come upon the scene. 'What's going on?' she asked.

Dr Challoner straightened up. 'Lynne's had a fall. It looks like a Colles fracture—typical dinner fork deformity,' he pointed out.

'Oh yes, typical,' nodded Wendy. She gave Lynne a sympathetic smile. 'Poor you! Shall we-er —what do you propose, Rob?'

He stroked his long straight nose, considering. 'Well, she's in no shape to have a general anaesthetic for a few hours, is she? We'd best get her to the hospital and put on a backslab for the time being. Then she can be X-rayed and have it properly reduced in the morning. How are you fixed for transport?' he asked, addressing the question to Charlotte.

'We came in my car. I can drive her there.'

'OK, I'll follow you in. Is there something we could use for a sling to make her arm more comfortable?' His eye fell on the silk square about Wendy's slim neck and she immediately pulled it off.

'Yes, do take this,' she said.

'Thanks, I'll see you get it back,' Charlotte promised.

'Sorry to be such a nuisance,' Lynne murmured faintly.

'Don't be silly—you're not.' Folding the scarf into a triangle, Charlotte cradled the injured arm in a comfortable position and tied the sling in place. 'How's that? Do you feel all right to walk to the car now?'

Lynne nodded, making an effort to control her trembling lips. She wriggled her foot into the shoe that had thrown her off balance. 'Yes, I'm fine,' she faltered, sounding anything but.

Robert patted her shoulder. 'We'll give you something for the pain as soon as we get there,' he promised.

As Charlotte took her friend's arm to lead her out to the car she overheard Wendy murmur, 'There's actually no need for you to go, you know, Rob. The casualty officer would be able to handle it.'

'Oh, I think we should look after her, don't you?' he returned. 'In any case, I may as well make myself known there. If you'd rather go home, I can drop you off on the way.'

'I wouldn't dream of deserting you, 'Wendy declared.

It seemed they had come in the one car and it was clear that this turn of events had rather spoiled Wendy's plans for the rest of the evening. But that was an occupational hazard in the medical world. However, it was perfectly true that Robert Challoner need not personally have involved himself, and Charlotte appreciated his concern. It would certainly be helpful to have his personal attention if the casualty department happened to be busy.

'Oh what a wretched nuisance,' Lynne groaned as she was helped into the car and her seat belt fastened. 'It's nice of Robert to bother, though, isn't it?'

'Well, if they can't look after the staff, for heaven's sake!' Charlotte retorted. She started up the car and they moved off. 'It looks like you'll be seeing your nice anaesthetist again sooner than you expected,' she added.

Lynne groaned once more. 'Oh dear! How embarrassing. Not exactly romantic to have him sticking an airway down my throat, although I couldn't care less about who does what at the moment. This arm is murder.'

'Grit your teeth, we'll soon be there,' Charlotte consoled.

As it happened, the casualty department was quiet that Sunday night. The emergency appendix operation for which Ken Jameson had been recalled was already in theatre, and the night staff were having their first coffee break.

Cheryl, the diminutive dark-haired duty Sister who had met Lynne on a number of occasions, greeted them in surprise. 'Hallo! What's happened to you?' she said.

Charlotte was explaining the situation when the two doctors also arrived. It was a very friendly gathering they had in one of the treatment rooms and, but for the fact that Lynne was in considerable pain, Charlotte would have enjoyed being back in the familiar hospital situation.

'There's obviously no point in calling out a radiographer at this hour,' Robert decided. 'Will you put a backslab on for now, Sister? And let's give her some pethidine . . .I'll write that up for you.'

'OK,' Cheryl handed him a treatment sheet 'and we may as well keep her in overnight. There's a bed in the day-room. That'll save her all the hassle of toing and fro-ing, won't it? Then we'll get the X-ray done first thing.'

'Fine. I'll look in tomorrow morning. Don't have any breakfast, will you?' Robert went on with a half-smile at Lynne.

'Food's the last thing on my mind,' she returned with a pained expression.

'I can imagine!' He penned his authority for the analgesic injection and handed it back to Cheryl. 'There you are. So we'll leave you to look after her, Sister.'

The doctors said goodnight and departed and Cheryl made preparations to give the prescribed pain relief. Having checked the ampoule with one of her staff, she drew it up into the syringe. 'Hop up on to the bed while I get this into you,' she said cheerfully. 'I think I'm going to like Dr Challoner. Seems to know what he's doing, doesn't he?' She wiped the injection site with a steri-swab, expelled the air from the syringe and pushed the needle into Lynne's thigh. 'Nice to work with someone who doesn't dither.'

'Mmm,' said Lynne without much enthusiasm. 'Not that I'll be doing much working with anyone for the next six weeks or so, shall I?'

'Never mind. Once you get it properly reduced and the swelling goes down you'll be able to use your fingers . . .in fact, you'll need to,' Charlotte added. 'Thank your lucky stars it wasn't your leg you broke. What will you do, go home?'

'Shan't be able to drive,' moaned Lynne.

'I'll take you.'

'We-ell, I'd probably be bored at home after a few

days. I might rather stick around, if I won't be too much of a nuisance.'

'You can talk about that later. Let's get on with this backslab and put you to bed before your legs give out.' Cheryl soaked plaster of Paris bandages and shaped a support to cushion the broken wrist, binding it neatly into position with dry open-wove bandages and supporting it in a sling. 'There, that all right? I'll get you a gown.'

After having seen Lynne settled for the night, and with promises to ring the District Nursing Officer to tell her about the accident, Charlotte drove home alone. It was gone one o'clock by the time she let herself into the silent house, mulling over the unexpected end to the evening.

Throwing off her party clothes, she brushed her teeth and rinsed her face before tumbling into bed. Although she was weary there were a million thoughts chasing round in her brain. Tomorrow she must remember to phone the DNO, and she would have to take in some daytime clothes for Lynne to come home in—she wouldn't feel right in last night's party gear.

Mondays were always busy at the Health Centre. In the morning there would be the routine injections and dressings, interspersed by calls from the doctors if they needed her assistance. Then in the afternoon there was the baby immunisation clinic. That was mostly a joy but apt to be time-consuming when mothers wanted to chat about everything from toilet training to troublesome teenagers or family problems.

Charlotte herself was barely twenty-five and to be

thought an authority on all things under the sun was quite a responsibility. The effect, she supposed, of her dark blue uniform which credited her with a wisdom beyond her years. She only wished she had instant solutions to half the problems that confronted people.

Certainly life in her present situation was far from boring, as her father had suggested. On the contrary, you could never tell what nice—or nasty—surprises it had in store. She couldn't quite make up her mind into which of those two categories Robert Challoner fitted. His strong, intelligent face swam before her, the blue eyes magnetic in their intensity. Obviously not married, or even attached, judging by his plea for help on the matter of decor. Of course, he might be divorced, or separated or between affairs. She hadn't gleaned anything about his social status when they first met, but she couldn't imagine a man of his undoubted appeal going through life like a monk.

When Charlotte arrived at the Health Centre the next day, the waiting-room was already well populated and a few familiar faces smiled at her.

Pausing at the reception desk, she greeted the motherly clerk who ran the practice with tact and efficiency: 'Good morning, Helen. Anything for me?'

'Here you are, dear.' Helen passed over a batch of patients' notes. 'Shame about Lynne last night, wasn't it? Did you get her fixed up all right?'

'Yes, they put on a temporary plaster and kept her in overnight. She's to have it set this morning. Which reminds me, I have to phone her DNO.'

Going through to her office, Charlotte hung her duffel coat in her locker and tidied her hair before making the necessary phone call. Then, in the adjoining treatment room, she placed a clean paper sheet on the examination couch and set out a dressings trolley in preparation for her first patient.

The morning's work covered a variety of things. There was a varicose ulcer to dress, injections to give, stitches for removal, an ear to syringe, and Wendy Fenner needed her assistance to suture a gaping cut on a child's knee.

Her last patient before lunch was Mrs Dent, a wheezy, overweight lady who had come for a cervical smear test.

'Hallo, Mrs Dent,' Charlotte greeted her with a smile and pointed to a chair. 'Sit down a minute while I make a few notes.' She asked the appropriate questions about age, and pregnancies, and the monthly cycle. 'And when did you last have a smear test?'

Oh, I never have. I don't have any problems down below, but my daughter says we all ought to have it done to be on the safe side.'

'She's right. Better to be sure than sorry,' Charlotte agreed. 'It's quite a painless process. Have we seen your daughter, then?'

'Yes . . .' The woman paused for a bout of coughing. 'Her name's Mrs Clifton. She lives next door to you, as a matter of fact.'

'Oh, Marjorie!' Charlotte exclaimed. 'With a little girl named Debby?'

'Yes, that's right. Do you want me to strip off for this?'

'Just your tights and pants—unless you'd like me to check your breasts as well.'

'OK, I may as well have the whole works while I'm here,' Mrs Dent agreed breathily.

'Well, that all looks nice and normal,' Charlotte reassured her, having taken the smear and transferred it to the glass slide. 'We'll send this off to the lab and we'll let you know the result in about a month.' She peeled off her disposable plastic gloves before checking for breast lumps. 'And no problems here—but you do sound wheezy. Are you just getting over a cold?'

'We-ell, I had one a couple of weeks back, but this is my normal smoker's cough . . .' Mrs Dent swung her legs over the side of the couch and began putting on her pants and tights.

Charlotte, washing her hands at the basin, turned to look at her. 'How many do you smoke?'

'About forty a day,'

'Do you? That's a bit heavy. Couldn't you try and cut it down?'

'I have tried once or twice, but—well—it's my only vice,' the woman laughed. 'I don't drink and I've never cheated on my husband . . .' She paused for another fit of coughing and Charlotte shook her head despairingly.

'Cigarettes kill thousands of people every year in this country, you know. Besides, think of all the lovely money you'd save if you gave up.'

'I know—I could have my kitchen modernised, couldn't I?' Mrs Dent joked.

On the spur of the moment Charlotte asked: 'Which doctor do you usually see?'

'Well, I haven't been to anyone for ages. Dr Bates it was, but she's left now, hasn't she?'

'Yes, Dr Challoner has taken over from her. Look while you're here, shall I get him to listen to your chest? I'll just see if he's available.' Picking up the internal phone before the patient could demur, she pressed the appropriate button and in a couple of seconds Robert Challoner answered.

'Yes?' he said.

The resonant voice sent a small thrill down her spine. 'Sister here. I've got a lady in the treatment room who's very chesty. I wondered if you could spare a minute to take a look at her?'

'Well, I'm rather tied up this morning. Can't you get her to make another appointment?'

'Oh couldn't you possibly fit her in while she's here?' Charlotte cajoled. 'She is one of yours . . .'

There was another short pause and an audible sigh. 'I thought you were meant to be a help, not a hindrance,' he lamented. 'I'll be along in a minute.'

'Thanks.' She put down the phone, privately hoping she had done the right thing. 'He won't be long, Mrs Dent. You'll like him, he's very nice.'

Robert Challoner gave her a cryptic glance when he strode into the treatment room a few minutes later. She returned him a honeyed smile and introduced the patient. 'She's got a persistent cough and it's some time since she had a check-up, so I thought . . .'.

'OK. Hallo, Mrs Dent,' he said, pleasantly enough. 'We'd better give you the once-over, then.' Fixing his stethoscope into his ears, he asked her to breathe deeply, and to cough, and whether she had pain anywhere.

'Not really—I just feel kind of heavy—and I do get a bit short of breath now and then.'

He sat on the edge of the couch, looking thoughtful after finishing his examination. 'Her blood pressure?' he asked, glancing up at Charlotte.

'Sorry, I haven't checked that.'

'Why not?' he queried briskly, reaching for the instrument sitting on the bottom of Charlotte's trolley and proceeding to make the test himself.

'Well, she came in for a cervical smear actually, not a general health check.'

'I see. Alright, Mrs Dent, I'd like you to have an X-ray to make sure we don't overlook anything. I'll give you a letter to take along to the hospital.'

'Oh—er—is that necessary?'

'We have to set Sister's mind at rest!' he said with a crooked smile. 'She worries about people. I'll leave the letter for you at the reception desk and you can collect it on your way out.' He picked up her notes and returned to his own office.

Chatting nervously, Mrs Dent proceeded to get dressed. 'Oh dear, I didn't think I'd end up being sent to hospital. Isn't it a lot of fuss about nothing? I mean, I'm only a bit bronchial. Some cough mixture would have done.'

Charlotte rinsed off the vaginal speculum she had used and placed it back in the steriliser. 'I expect the doctor is being extra thorough, not having seen you before, and it can't do any harm, can it? If anything does show up on the X-ray they'll be able to do something about it. You will go, won't you?'

'Suppose I won't be able to show my face here

again if I don't' Mrs Dent laughed.

'Too right!' Charlotte returned with mock severity, 'and would you like to have a look through these?' She handed over some leaflets giving advice on how to stop smoking. 'If you'd really like to try to give up, maybe they will help.'

Her next task was to phone the hospital to ask about Lynne.

'She's fine—back in the day ward sleeping off her anaesthetic at the moment,' the staff nurse told her. 'She'll be ready to leave later this afternoon, as soon as she's steady on her pins.'

'OK, thanks. I'll be in to collect her,' Charlotte promised.

Having tidied her treatment room ready for the afternoon baby clinic, she put on her coat and went out into the corridor, past the consulting rooms, intent on a quick visit to the supermarket to buy some groceries and a pack of sandwiches for her lunch. Black medical bag in hand, Robert Challoner emerged from his surgery and followed close behind her, en route for his house calls.

She gave him a shy smile as he caught her up and held open the door for her. 'Thank you for seeing Mrs Dent. Was there anything . . .?'

'She certainly needs looking into,' he allowed, 'but it would have waited, she could have made another appointment.'

'The trouble is, she might not have bothered. She's probably been neglecting herself for years. No time like the present, is there?' she added brightly.

The dazzling blue eyes looking steadily into hers held a glint of amusement. 'Hmm. Well, I'm glad to find *you* picked yourself up and bounced back again.'

Her mouth dropped open. She flashed him a startled look and blushed. 'Sorry?'

'We have met before, you know. St Chad's—night duty?'

'Oh, so you did remember me.' She laughed self-consciously. 'I-I was hoping you hadn't.'

'Were you? Why?'

Charlotte wrinkled her nose. 'We-ell, you must have thought I was a drip that night. I mean I was really pathetic—something I would rather forget about. And there was I thinking you were miles away. Didn't it work out for you in Canada?'

'Oh, that. I was only making a private visit, not taking up residence. As a matter of fact, I found your bounce-back attitude quite thought-provoking. Which was why I remembered you,' he explained.

Finding herself the focus of his steady gaze was disconcerting. 'Really?' she murmured. 'It's funny the things which stick in one's mind.'

'So what you brought you to Yorkshire? Putting the miles between you and the two-timing boyfriend?'

'No, I simply fancied a change of scene. This job attracted me, and it's nearer my home.'

'Ah! So the dragon aunt has mellowed, has she?'

Charlotte laughed. 'Actually, she got *married!* And your memory is far too long, Dr Challoner. 'Bye!' She went on her way to the shops.

Throughout the rest of the busy day the conversation came back to her. Well, it had a least cleared the air between them if nothing else. And she wasn't unique in having had a calamitous romance, or a fraught childhood. The fact that he'd waited until they were alone before raising the subject pointed to his discretion. All the same, she couldn't help feeling somewhat exposed by his reappearance in her life.

By four o'clock Charlotte was treating her last little patient—a chubby nine-months-old baby girl—for her final injection of the triple vaccine against diphtheria, tetanus and whooping cough. 'All over, sweetheart,' she murmured as the infant let out a howl of protest.

Young Mrs Gordon, whose first child it was, gave the infant a cuddle. 'Poor little pet. I was a bit worried about letting her have the one for whooping cough. I mean, you do hear about things going wrong sometimes, don't you?'

'Not in normally healthy babies like Holly,' Charlotte reassured her. 'There's usually some contributary factor which has been overlooked, such as epilepsy in the family, or the baby having had fits. We checked that there are no problems like that in your family, and whooping cough itself is a serious illness. It can have all sorts of nasty complications.' She filled in the baby's record card and handed it to the girl. 'That should keep her protected until she's ready to start school. We'll send you a reminder next year when it's time for her measles jab.'

'OK, and thanks, Nurse.'

Mrs Gordon went off with her rosy-cheeked infant warmly dressed in a pink woolly pram-suit, and Charlotte could not help an envious sigh. It must be wonderful, she thought, to have a warm little bundle of your own to love. But that entailed finding the right man to share your life, and the whole complicated minefield of human passions which that involved. After Phil she had made up her mind it wasn't worth the hassle.

CHAPTER THREE

A MONTH had passed since Lynne had first fractured her wrist. It had been a busy time for Charlotte, with her friend being virtually one-handed and needing assistance in many ways. Now, her last X-ray having confirmed that the broken bones were still in correct alignment and uniting well, Lynne had decided to go home for a spell.

'Home' was near Buxton in Derbyshire, some two hours' drive away, and Ken Jameson had offered to take her. The hospital anaesthetist had been a regular visitor to the house in Spinney Lane since Lynne's fall. His first call one evening shortly after the accident was to make good his promise of showing them the crude surgical instruments his great-grandfather had used during the Crimean War. Since then Charlotte was no longer suprised to find his tall, gangling figure on their doorstep.

Sometimes the three of them went out to the Cross Keys Inn, their friendly local tavern. At other times, Charlotte tactfully excused herself, seeing the way things were shaping between the other two.

'You don't mind Ken taking me home, do you?' Lynne asked that Friday evening as Charlotte helped her with her packing. 'I mean, I know you did offer . . .'

'Of course I don't mind.' Laughing, Charlotte

zipped up the bulging travel bag. I'll come and collect you if you like—unless you want Ken to do that as well.'

'Oh, I'll play that by ear, Lotty. Mustn't appear too eager, must I?'

'You really like him, don't you?' Charlotte sat back on her heels and gave her friend an understanding grin.

Lynne sighed. 'I'm in love!' she confessed, dreamy-eyed. 'And he seems quite keen, don't you think?'

'Mmm,' Charlotte agreed dryly, 'you wouldn't have to be clairvoyant to spot that.'

'He's quite shy really, you know,' Lynne told her.

'Well, that makes a nice change. They usually can't wait to get you into bed,' Charlotte returned. 'You play it cool.'

'Was that where you went wrong last time?' her friend wanted to know.

Charlotte gave a noncommittal shrug. Lynne knew none of the distressing details of her affair with Phil, only that she had left a broken romance behind her in London. She had relived the bitter break-up so often in her quiet moments, she preferred not to talk about it. That would only serve to resurrect the past. And for all of her efforts to the contrary, there was still an enormous ache in her heart when she thought of him.

Now she said: 'I suppose I m ay have been a bit obvious, but when you're in love with someone it's only natural you want to show it.'

'Yes, I know what you mean,' Lynne agreed. 'You've never said much about him, except that he was a cas officer. What was he like?'

'Oh, good-looking—clever—bags of charm. I couldn't believe my luck when he fancied me. He could have had anyone. He'd told me he was divorced, but it turned out that it wasn't true. They were just living apart. She discovered she was pregnant and wanted him back.'

'You were well out of it then, Lotty,' Lynne returned. They were both silent for a moment, then she went on, 'I don't think Ken would be like that. He's got a really lovely nature, hasn't he?'

Charlotte smiled and nodded. 'Yes, he seems a really nice guy.'

'He talks a lot about his family,' Lynne rattled on. 'They live near Windermere. He said we might have a weekend there when I get rid of my plaster.'

'Well, that won't be long now. A couple more weeks and you'll have two decent hands to defend yourself with,' Charlotte teased.

'Yeah. Thanks for putting up with me all this time. I'll do as much for you one day?'

'I hope you never have to!' The doorbell interrupted their confidences. 'That sounds like your chauffeur. Come on!' Charlotte picked up her friend's bag and carried it downstairs.

After the cold early start to the year, May was now making amends for frequent bursts of warm sunshine. The daffodils had gone, to be replaced by starry primroses in the hedgerows and the sheen of bluebells in woodland places. At eight p.m. it was still light and bright when Charlotte waved Lynne and Ken on their way.

She paused at the gate to enjoy the scents of spring on the evening air and to admire the rosy clumps of Primula Wanda along the border. It promised to be a fine weekend. On Saturday mornings she didn't go to the practice, her treatment room being covered by a married part-time nurse. With Lynne being away, Charlotte had decided she ought to take the opportunity to go home and see her father again.

'Ah, sorry, lass,' John Blythe said when she rang him, 'full day tomorrow. I'm sending some stock to market. Can't say what time I'll be back. You know how it is when you get meeting folks . . .'

Charlotte smiled to herself, picturing the groups of farmers in country tweeds swapping news and views over a friendly pint in the local. It was what her father enjoyed, a yarn with men of like mind, for all he complained about the hazards of farming.

'Right, Dad, I'll swing it this time. Maybe next weekend. I'll let you know. Enjoy yourself—hope you do well at the market.'

She put down the phone with a slight feeling of disappointment. He had shown no interest in anything she might be doing. But then he seldom did, so that was nothing new. Even after all these years, though, she was still hurt by the reminder that she was not the son he had wanted. A son would have been able to join him at the market and yarn with him over that pint.

Oh well, she thought with a philosophical shrug, she was never at a loss for things to do, and her circle of friends was growing. Tomorrow night, for instance, there was a barbecue and barn dance at the Cross Keys Inn that she was now free to go to. Bryan

Dalgleish had particularly mentioned it when she went into the chemist's for some shampoo. He'd asked if she would be going, and if so could he pick her up? At the time she had not committed herself. She had an idea that Bryan's interest was more than just friendly, and although she liked him that was as far as it went for Charlotte. But she could face that problem if ever it arose. No need to miss out on a good social evening

Her thoughts were interrupted by another ring at the front door. She opened it to find nine-year-old Debby Clifton from next door, dressed in her Brownie uniform. She was a rosy-cheeked child with long straight brown hair, and her wide hazel eyes were anxious.

Charlotte gave her a warm smile. She had come to know the family better since her dealings with Mrs Dent, the grandmother. 'Hallo, pet,' she said, 'what can I do for you?'

'It's me mam, she's poorly,' returned the little girl. 'She wondered if you'd got anything for an upset stomach?'

'Oh dear!' Charlotte sympathised. 'What kind of an upset stomach? Has she been sick?'

Debby nodded solemnly. ' . . . and she's got the tummy-ache.'

'I think I'd better come and see her.' Pausing to pick up her doorkey, Charlotte put her arm around the youngster's shoulders, asking questions as they went.

'Did it come on suddenly?'

'I don't know. I went to tea with my friend Pauline straight from school. Then we went to

Brownies together,' Debby confided, 'and when I got home Mam was lying on the bed. I made her some tea, but she didn't fancy it.'

There were sounds of the cistern being flushed as they went into the house. 'Shall I come up, Marjorie?' Without waiting for an answer Charlotte ran swiftly up the stairs and met her neighbour coming ashen-faced from the bathroom. The woman tottered into her bedroom, where she collapsed on the side of the bed, clutching her midriff, her face screwed up with pain.

Marjorie Clifton was a busy young mother in her mid-thirties, who worked full-time for an estate agent as well as running a home. Normally she appeared cheerful enough despite her constant dashing about. Now she passed a trembling hand over her clammy face and murmured, on sighing breaths, 'Oh dear . . . oh dear!'

'How long have you been like this, love?' Charlotte asked in concern.

'I've been feeling rotten all day, really. It came on worse when I got home from work . . . think I must've eaten something . . . and I feel so dizzy.'

She rested her head in her hands and Charlotte noticed the paper-white state of her fingernails. There was also a trace of reddish-brown on her chin. 'Was it food you brought up just now?' she queried.

'No just some sort of—liquid stuff.'

'Like coffee grounds?'

'Yes, I suppose it was. S-sorry to bother you, only I thought, with you being a nurse, you'd know the best thing to take . . .'

'We ought to find out first what's causing it,

Marjorie. It doesn't seem like an ordinary bilious attack to me.' Charlotte knelt down and took off her neighbour's slippers. 'Why don't you lie down? It'll help to stop you feeling faint.' She drew the duvet over the sick woman, checked her pulse and went on in a soothing voice, 'I shouldn't try to get up again —Debby can bring you a basin in case you feel sick. I'm going to call the doctor. Come on, Debby you show me where your telephone is.'

'It's in our front room.' Debby bounded eagerly down the stairs and showed her to the deep windowsill in the square bay where their telephone sat. 'I'll get the basin,' she said , darting off towards the kitchen. She was a helpful little girl, the armful of badges on her uniform was evidence of her enthusiasm, and Charlotte felt she was probably glad of being given something useful to do.

Dialling the group practice number, she wondered who was on call. The Centre itself would be closed at this time of night, but the line would be switched through to whoever was on standby. Charlotte had no idea who that would be.

'Dr Challoner here.' The deeply resonant voice caused her inside to lurch. Her dealings with the doctor had been harmonius to date and she hoped to keep it that way. There had been no further reference to their past encounter, but she still felt a little in awe of him because of it. She hoped she would not be guilty of calling him out unnecessarily, although she would gladly be proved wrong for Marjorie's sake.

Taking a deep breath, she pushed aside her personal qualms and began to explain. 'Robert, this is Charlotte. It's about my next-door neighbour. I'm afraid she may have had a gastric bleed. It seems like a haematemesis although I didn't actually see it, but she looks grey and her pulse rate's over one hundred. I think she should be visited as a matter of urgency.'

'I see.' There was a momentary pause, then Robert went on. 'Well, if that's your opinion, all right, Charlotte, I'll be there as soon as I can. Address?'

Having given him the details, she went back to reassure the patient. 'Dr Challoner's coming to see you. He's the one who saw your mother. Who do you usually see?'

'Dr McAllister. Not that I've been to see him much for myself—it's been more for Debs . . .' Marjorie murmured faintly. Lying on her side with her knees drawn up, she groaned: 'Oh God! I feel terrible. Can't be my appendix—I had that out when I was fourteen.'

'Let's get you undressed,' Charlotte prompted. 'That'll make it easier for the doctor to look at you.' She smiled at the little Brownie hovering nearby. 'Debby, will you find me your mummy's nightie?'

Fifteen minutes later Robert Challoner had arrived and Charlotte discreetly took the little girl downstairs while the doctor made his examination.

Presently he joined them in the living-room where he had a kindly smile for the youngster. 'OK, Debby, you can go back and see your mummy while I make some arrangements.'

With the child out of earshot, Charlotte queried: 'Well?'

Resting his medical bag on the table, Robert clicked it open. 'Yes, I imagine it's as you thought, a sharp gastric bleed. Apparently she's been under a lot of stress lately—taking a good many aspirins, so that may be the cause. Did you know her husband had left her?'

Charlotte's soft green eyes widened. 'Oh! No, I didn't. We don't know the family awfully well. We don't see much of them . . .'

'Well, she doesn't want her husband told—she's adamant about that,' Robert declared. 'We must get her admitted as an emergency tonight somewhere.' He nodded in the direction of the telephone. 'Will you get me the Valley Hospital? Let's hope they've got a bed.'

While Charlotte got through to the hospital he searched out a sheet of notepaper and began writing his explanatory letter. Before long satisfactory arrangements had been made and an ambulance ordered.

'Poor Debby,' Charlotte said, her thoughts straying back many years to another small girl whose mother had been ill, 'I hope Mrs Clifton's going to be all right.'

'With prompt attention there's every reason to think she will be. Lucky you were on the spot,' observed Robert, finishing his letter and sealing it in an envelope.

Charlotte gave an uncertain smile. 'So I was justified in calling you. I was almost prepared for a rocket.'

'Come, come!' he said in mild rebuke. 'You should have more faith in yourself. I'd rather be called out unnecessarily than too late.'

'That's what I thought,' she returned, her cheeks flushing.

'Well, now you know. And what are we going to do about this child? She can't stay here alone,' the doctor went on.

'No . . .' Charlotte frowned, 'there are some grandparents. Do you remember Mrs Dent? You sent her for chest X-rays.'

He cast his mind back. 'Oh, that lady. Yes, there were no intractable problems, fortunately. I put her on antibiotics for the bronchitis."

'Fine. So she might be able to take Debby,' Charlotte said hopefully. 'Failing that, she can stay here with me for the night, and we'll get in touch with the social services tomorrow. Anyway, I'll take her with me to the hospital when they come for Marjorie. She'll be less worried if she knows where her mother is.'

Robert Challoner replaced his ballpoint in his inside jacket pocket and regarded this friend in need somewhat quizzically. She had the problem sorted, and no hint of a grumble about any personal inconvenience. He was impressed, in spite of himself. Not that one act of kindness set her apart from the rest of her capricious sex, did it?

His impassive expression revealed none of his thoughts and Charlotte gave him an apprehensive smile. 'That sound OK to you?'

'Yes, if you think you can cope,' he said, almost curtly. 'I'll leave it with you,then. If you get into difficulties you must let me know.' He handed her the letter, picked up his medical bag, said goodnight and let himself out of the house. Robert Challoner did not enjoy having his considered opinions undermined.

With much to be done Charlotte had no time to bother unduly about the doctor's distant manner. She just assumed that he was busy and that she had added to his workload. Not that it hadn't been justified, as he himself had admitted.

Running back up to the bedroom, she told her sick neighbour what had been decided, reassured Debby that her mother would be in the best possible place and, with the child's help, put together a few essential items to go with the patient. Next she telephoned Mrs Dent who was naturally concerned and said she would gladly look after her granddaughter.

'So that's all fixed, Marjorie,' Charlotte comforted. 'When the ambulance comes for you, Debby and I will follow on in my car, and your mother will meet us at the hospital.' The child was beginning to look apprehensive and her bottom lip started to quiver. Charlotte gave her a quick cuddle. 'All right, sweetheart? You stick with me until we see your gran. And your mummy may not be away for too long. Come on, let's pack a nightie and a toothbrush for you, too,' she encouraged.

Both Mrs Dent and her husband arrived at the Casualty Department within minutes of their daughter being taken there. Charlotte stayed to talk to them while the medical registrar went through the preliminaries. Marjorie was put on a saline drip and X-rayed and then admitted for further investigation.'

Having done all she could, and satisfied that Debby was in good hands, Charlotte felt free to return home. It was ten-thirty before she got back to Spinney Lane, where she was immediately approached by another neighbour out walking her dog.

'I saw the ambulance,' Mrs Briggs said curiously. 'Was that Mrs Clifton they took away?'

'Yes . . . some gastric trouble. She's gone to hospital for investigation.'

'Dear me!' the woman tutted, shaking her head. 'Keeps herself to herself, Mrs Clifton does, but if there's aught I can do . . . I mean, what about the bairn?'

'Oh, she's gone to stay with her grandparents.'

'That's all right, then. Only I shouldn't like to think that there was no one to look after her. After all, what are neighbours for?'

'True,' Charlotte smiled, her hand on the gate.

'Lucky you was living next door, with you being a nurse. I'd a mind to have a word with you myself, about my husband's waterworks . . . takes him ages to go,' the woman confided. 'I reckon it's a stricture, but he won't do anything about it. Is there something you can buy at the chemist's for that?'

'We-ell,' Charlotte demurred, 'he'd be far better off going to see his doctor. It could be due to any number of things.' She was getting used to being recognised and stopped in the street and asked to recommend instant cures for anything from hammer toes to halitosis.

On the pretext that she was expecting a phone

call, Charlotte said goodnight and disappeard with some relief behind her own front door. It was true that her work as a practice nurse was more routine and less dramatic than the crises with which she had often been faced in hospital, but living within the community it was only too easy to get involved in people's domestic problems. Sadly, a sympathetic ear was sometimes all she could offer.

Sighing, she went into the kitchen and filled the kettle to make herself a hot drink. It was after eleven now, and when the door bell rang she jumped and took the precaution of putting on the chain-lock before answering.

To her suprise, Robert Challoner's powerful frame met her gaze. 'Saw your light,' he said with a brief smile, 'so I knew you were still up.'

'Oh!' She was nonplussed. 'Er—will you come in?' She released the chain and held open the door, meeting his mesmeric blue eyes with a look of enquiry.

Stepping into the tiny hall, he seemed to fill most of the space available. 'I've just come from the hospital,' he told her. 'Professor Frith will be seeing Mrs Clifton in the morning. Meantime they're getting her cross-matched and on to some blood, which should improve matters for the time being. You managed to fix up the youngster, did you?'

His deep voice and discerning gaze sparked disquieting bodily responses in Charlotte. In a way he was similar to Phil, she thought. One of nature's darlings, with that effortless charm which seduced the senses. Well, she had seen it all before, and she was not so naïve now.

'Yes,' she replied, 'her grandparents were only to pleased to have her.' Pushing a hand through her tumbled fair hair, Charlotte was suddenly very conscious of her homespun image. In faded jeans and a red sweatshirt she felt at a disadvantage, being alone with the personable Robert Challoner at this late hour. Earlier in the evening she had been too preoccupied to give her appearance a second thought. 'Um . . .' she hesitated, swallowing, 'I was just going to make a coffee. Would you like one?'

It seemed the hospitable thing to say, but she half expected him to decline. He didn't; he followed her into the kitchen and perched on a stool while she prepared it. 'Where's your stablemate tonight?' he asked.

'Lynne? Oh, she's gone home for a while, to relieve the monotony.'

'I see. Yes, it's tedious being put out of action.'

Charlotte reached for the coffee jar and made the drinks. She couldn't imagine what had really brought him back, unless it was to satisfy himself about Debby. But he could have asked about that at the hospital, couldn't he? And if the inquisitive Mrs Briggs had noticed his car outside, goodness knows what *she* would make of it. 'Come and have a comfortable seat,' she said, putting the mugs on a tray.

She led the way into the living-room where he draped his long frame into one of the chintz-covered easy chairs and glanced around him with interest. There was an old-fashioned oak sideboard with a gilt-framed mirror over it, some ladderback dining chairs and an oval gate-legged dining table, all pieces that Lynne had picked up cheaply in secondhand shops from time to time. The house now had central heating and on the empty natural stone hearth Charlotte had place a brown Toby jug full of sweet-smelling wallflowers. The overall impression was cottagey and welcoming.

'Do you rent this furnished?' he wanted to know.

'No—Lynne's buying it. My rent helps towards her mortgage. Sugar?' She pushed the bowl of brown crystals towards him and he helped himself liberally.

'I've got a sweet tooth, I'm afraid.'

Charlotte sat cross-legged on the floor with her back against one of the other chairs. 'We all have our weaknesses.'

'So what are yours?' he asked, watching her idly.

She shook her head and gave a light laugh. 'Oh no! This is not going to be another night of confessions.'

'No?' The corners of his mouth twitched. 'Pity. I was looking forward to some more startling revelations.'

'I wish you wouldn't remind me of that night,' she returned. 'You just happened to catch me in an off moment. Apart from changing my job, life has been quite unspectacular since then. How about yours?' she demanded, meeting his steady gaze boldly. 'You never did explain why you changed from computers to medicine.'

'Oh, you remembered that, did you? Well, I suppose it was because I was on the receiving end for some months, which changed my sense of values.'

He had one long leg propped across the other,

exposing part of his bare skin, and Charlotte caught a glimpse of extensive scarring. She nodded towards it. 'Was it anything to do with that?'

With a strained smile he pulled down his trouser leg to cover the damage. 'Yes. I fell off the side of a mountain. Came near to losing the damn thing, and my life, actually. But here I am, ninety-nine per cent whole and a living testimony to modern medicine.'

'Which mountain, and how did you come to fall off?' she persisted.

'It was Ben Nevis. I was on a climbing weekend. I slipped—I was careless—nothing more sinister than that.' Abruptly he changed the subject by getting up to peer at a watercolour on an artist's pad, propped up against the wall on the sideboard. It was a local scene which Charlotte had painted when the daffodils were in bloom.

'C. Blythe,' he read, deciphering her signature at the bottom. 'Did you do this?'

'Yes. Lynne likes it, so I'm going to get it framed for her.'

Robert came to sit down again. 'That's quite a talent' he remarked. 'So that's how you spend your spare time, is it?'

'Some of it.'

'Is that what you'll be doing this weekend—or is that also none of my business?'

She laughed. 'My life's an open book. There's a barbecue and barn dance at the Cross Keys tomorrow, so I'll probably go to that, if it's fine. I was going home, but my dad has to be away on farm business. So much for his talk about selling up since there's no one to take over the farm when he retires,' she added drily.

Robert raised a dark eyebrow. 'You could always provide him with a lusty, eligible son-in-law from one of these Young Farmers' Clubs. I should have thought you would be a hot marriageable property.'

'Perish the thought!' Charlotte retorted. 'If I ever marry, it won't be for that reason. I'm perfectly happy doing my own thing. Who needs the hang-ups of matrimony?'

The doctor smiled and shook his head in a paternalistic fashion. 'Cynicism in one so young? But I agree—the single life is far less complicated, isn't it? You're a girl after my own heart.' He finished his drink. 'Well, I'll away and let you get your beauty sleep.'

'Yes, I think you better had, or my reputation will be in shreds if my nosey neighbour has spotted your car,' she grinned.

They bade each other a pleasant goodnight and, after seeing him to the door, Charlotte dumped the coffee mugs in the sink and went up to bed. Sleep, however, was another matter. What was all that about? She wondered. It had been a puzzling interlude between the doctor and herself. She couldn't exactly fathom why he had come back to see her.

Maybe he had just felt like talking—unwinding after a demanding day—with someone who understood the pressures of his job. In that case she supposed she should feel flattered, and she had to admit that she did find him fascinating. But as a successful and popular doctor he was hardly likely to be short of people to talk to, so why pick on her? If it was female company he fancied, why not Wendy, who was nearer his age, and had plenty in common with him and made no secret of the fact that she liked him? Unless, of course, in the same way as she felt about Bryan, Robert didn't want to encourage Wendy.

Maybe it was knowing Charlotte's history, and the greater difference in their ages, which made him feel on safe ground with her? All very satisfactory from a work point of view, but hardly flattering, she thought with a self-mocking smile.

It suddenly occurred to her that he hadn't known she was going to be alone at the house tonight. He'd been suprised that Lynne wasn't around. So it was probably just a friendly, spur-of-the-moment visit, thinking they would both be there. Safety in numbers, and Charlotte was making a great mystery out of nothing, wasn't she? The discovery made her feel oddly crestfallen. Not that she cared two pins about how Robert Challoner wished to conduct his private life!

CHAPTER FOUR

THE WEEKEND turned out to be entirely different from Charlotte's expectations. Saturday started with an unexpected and disturbing telephone call from a London solicitor. After introducing himself he went on to say that Dr Philip Erskine had named her to witness for him in an impending court case.

Her stomach lurched at the sound of Phil's name and yet another reminder of the days she was doing her best to forget. Much to her relief she learned it had nothing to do with Phil's matrimonial affairs. He and St Chad's Hospital were being sued for negligence by the wife of a patient who had died.

Charlotte remembered the incident well. She had been working with Phil in A & E on the night in question and the department had been full of drunks and druggies. She had helped him stitch up a deep scalp wound on a man who's been slashed with a meat cleaver. Although there was no skull fracture and no loss of consciousness, Phil had rightly ordered that the casualty should be admitted for observation.

The patient—a foul-mouthed obnoxious character—refused even to consider it. He also refused point-blank to sign the self-discharge form, and, against all advice, had been whisked away by the equally objectionable mates who had brought him in. A week later the man had died from a subdural haematoma.

Thinking back to that night, Charlotte swallowed nervously. Agreeing to give evidence would obviously mean her having to see Phil again. On the other hand, he was an excellent doctor and had done all in his power for the man. She had no wish to see him professionally harmed for the sake of an obscene lout who'd refused to accept advice.

'I-Is it absolutely necessary for me to be there?' she ventured. 'I mean, it is rather a long way to come, and there were other people who knew what happened . . .'

'I understand that you were the senior nurse assisting Dr Erskine at the time. You are a vital witness,' the solicitor explained. He paused, 'If it would help, for whatever reason, we can subpoena you.'

'Oh, we-ell, if you feel it's that important, of course I'll come,' she agreed. 'I know Dr Erskine wasn't in any way to blame for what happened.'

'Thank you, Miss Blythe. My client will be most grateful.' The solicitor advised her that her expenses would be met, '. . . both travel and accommodation should you need to stay overnight.' He went on to give her details of time and place and said he would confirm in writing.

When they had finished talking, Charlotte sat on for a while, chin in hands, gazing forlornly out at the sun-dappled front garden. Why did it have to be *me* working with Phil on that particular night? she mourned. The trouble was that she had adored working with him and did so whenever she could.

Working together was just an added bonus of the time they could share. Bodies brushing in confined spaces, intimate glances, even being jointly involved in high drama, all added to their heightened awareness of each other. That was until her rude awakening.

It was strange, she thought, how the past had suddenly come alive again. First with Robert Challoner turning up to join the practice, and now this. And since the case was due to be heard the following Friday, that meant she would have to tell Robert about it, to explain her absence from work. Which in turn would jog *his* memory about St Chad's and her unfortunate love affair there.

When the telephone rang again she picked it up absently, still preoccupied.

'It's going to be a fine night!' a deep male voice informed her.

Charlotte frowned, then came back to the present. 'Oh, hallo, Robert!' She made an effort to speak lightly. 'What is this, your own personal weather forecasting service?'

'That's right,' the doctor said cheerfully. 'I'm looking out across the meadow and all the cows are standing up!'

She laughed. 'Very convincing! So what?'

'You spoke about going to that barbecue at the Cross Keys Inn if it were fine. I mentioned it to Wendy and we both rather fancied the idea. I wondered if we could give you a lift?'

Ah! Was he merely being friendly, or was this his safety-in-numbers ploy? She could not help a private smile, but some perverse streak in her made her turn down his offer. Socialising with a man as attractive as Robert could be courting trouble! Even small doses of his company she was beginning to find addictive, and she didn't want to risk getting emotionally involved again. Far better to keep things on a safe working basis.

'Thanks for the thought, Robert,' she said, 'but I am going with someone, actually.' Well, she had sort of promised to join Bryan's party if she went, hadn't she?

'Oh! Fair enough,' he replied airily. 'We may see you there, then.'

Was it her imagination that he sounded put out? 'Me and half the town, from what I hear,' she quipped.

'I see. So you're not likely to be short of company, I take it?'

He certainly did sound a bit disgruntled. She took no notice and returned sweetly, 'It's a very popular do, I believe. I'm sure you'll enjoy it.'

'With my luck,' he growled, 'someone will throw a coronary the minute *I* arrive.'

Charlotte chuckled. 'Then you'll be the hero of the hour, won't you, doctor?'

'Well, this doctor has better things to do than hold inane conversations with flippant females,' he retorted. 'Bye.'

Replacing the receiver slowly, she made a face at the phone. Whatever his intentions it would do him no harm to know that she could manage her own social life perfectly well, thank you. All the same, a show of pique from him was the last thing she needed, with Phil and his problem already on her mind.

Sighing heavily, Charlotte wished that Lynne was there to talk to. For all her apparent scattiness at times, Lynne could be relied upon to be logical and practical when the need arose. At that moment Charlotte herself felt anything but logical and practical; she felt like an insignificant pawn in the game of life. Picking up the telephone, she began dialling Lynne's home number. Then she stopped, remembering that Ken had been going to stay overnight at Lynne's home, which might make it inconvenient for a long heart-to-heart. So there was nothing to do but to fall back on her own initiative.

Firstly, she had to sort out the details of when to travel and where to stay in London. She decided to ring Amy, a good friend from her training days. Amy also had moved from St Chad's but she was still London based.

'Yes, of course, Lotty,' Amy enthused when Charlotte explained about the court case and asked could she have a bed for the night, 'it'll be really terrific to see you again . . .'

They chatted on for a time about the doings of various mutual friends, and Charlotte was reminded that, on the whole, the good times had outweighed the bad in her memories of the big city. As student nurses—many of them far from home—they had become interdependent, their small immediate circle more like a family. They had shared each other's highs and lows. In a way she missed the comradeship of those days, and she did not yet have that *belonging* feeling here in Niddborough. But you could not go back, only forward. At least joining in with Bryan's party tonight would be a step in the right direction.

With the best intentions in the world of shelving her problems and being sparkling and outgoing that evening, Charlotte found herself in a curious two-tier state of mind. Her body went through the motions of being sociable, but her thoughts were elsewhere.

It wasn't that there was any lack of atmosphere at the Cross Keys Inn. Fairy lights glowed in the trees surrounding the gardens, a suckling pig roasted on the spit over glowing embers, and a folk group provided lively background music. Bryan knew a great many people and Charlotte soon found herself being introduced to half the local cricket team who were celebrating after winning the first match of the season.

Having dined well on roast pork and jacket potatoes, they sat at a rustic table enjoying the music and company. Presently Bryan pointed out some late arrivals and said, 'There are two of your doctors . . . did you know they were coming?'

Charlotte's pulse quickened when she turned her head to see Robert with Wendy Fenner. She drank the last of her mulled wine in an attempt to preserve her composure. 'Yes, they did say they might,' she said.

'Let's go and say hallo.' Bryan drained his own glass and stood up, holding out his hand to her. 'Come on.'

She would have much preferred to stay where she was, get lost in the crowd, but Bryan was a friendly soul and so she had to arouse equal enthusiasm.

Wendy, looking elegant as ever although casually dressed, waited by the bar table while Robert ordered drinks. Tonight she wore white designer jeans and a stylish cerise overshirt, her dark hair caught back on the crown of her head with a decorative slide.

'Hi!' Bryan greeted her heartily. 'I didn't know this was a haunt of yours?'

'*Hallo*!' Wendy's warm smile included them both. 'Actually it isn't, but Robert persuaded me this might be fun.'

Robert joined them, drinks in hand, his shrewd blue eyes looking from one to the other, 'Hallo, you two! Can I get you something?'

'No, thanks,' Charlotte said, not wanting to prolong the meeting, 'We've wined and dined already, haven't we, Bry?'

'Yeah,' the pharmacist draped a possessive arm around her shoulders, 'we just popped over to say hallo before we get bopping.'

They stayed to exchange a few pleasantries, then Robert cast a satirical smile in Charlotte's direction. 'Well, don't let us keep you from the fun,' he said. 'Off you go and enjoy yourselves.'

Bryan chuckled. 'Sounds like a good idea, does that. We'll leave you to get some food, then. See you later. C'm on, Charlie,' and he whisked her off to mingle with the company already warming to the action.

Charlotte expended a great deal of energy and persuaded herself she was having a fabulous time. She even flirted with Bryan in a harmless sort of way, but resisted his invitation to go with his rambling club to Bolton Abbey the following day.

'Sorry, Bryan,' she told him, sitting in his car outside her house much later that night. 'If I went to Bolton Abbey I'd rather take my sketch book with me and stay there.'

'I could always sit and watch you.' His fresh-complexioned face broke into a grin. 'I could watch you for hours, no problem.'

She laughed. 'I thought the idea of a rambling club was to ramble? I'm not into all that healthy outdoors exercise.'

His lips twitched humorously. 'Very good for the libido, communing with nature. Ah well, unfortunately I can't duck out of it myself this time, seeing as I suggested it, but another time, perhaps?'

'Yes, maybe,' she said. 'See you, Bryan, and thanks for a lovely evening. It was really great.'

He raised a speculative eyebrow. 'What, no coffee?'

Charlotte smiled and shook her head. 'Too late. You need to conserve your strength for that walk tomorrow, don't you?'

'And there was I thinking I was on to a good thing tonight,' he grinned.

She wrinkled her nose at him. 'Men!' she said, and she wasn't only thinking of Bryan. They'd had no more contact with the doctors after that first greeting, but Charlotte had been well aware when the two of them left the inn. 'Wendy and Robert didn't stay long,' she observed. 'Maybe they had their own idea of fun.'

'Mmm—she's quite tasty, Wendy Fenner. I prefer blondes meself though, Charlie.' Bryan ruffled her honey locks playfully.

'Well, if you want us to stay friends, *don't* call me that,' she warned.

'Why, what's wrong with Charlie?'

'Oh, I detest it. Lotty, if you like.'

'OK, Lotty it is.' His eyes narrowed. 'Do you know, that's the first time I've got a real reaction from you tonight? Half the time you've been somewhere else.'

It was true; her thoughts had been alternating between Phil and Robert Challoner most of the evening. 'Have I? Sorry about that, Bryan, I did have things on my mind,' she admitted. 'Tell you about it some other time.'

He pulled her towards him for a goodnight kiss which, although pleasant, did absolutely nothing to stir her blood. The sight of Robert and Wendy leaving the Cross Keys Inn together had been more disturbing. Robert's manner that evening had been rather condescending, she thought; quite different from their intimate coffee-drinking session of the previous night. Oh well, if that was how he wanted to play it, fine. Familiarity was best avoided as far as she was concerned. No danger then of feelings getting out of control.

Charlotte had planned to spend a relaxing day on Sunday, but her lie-in was spoiled by thoughts of the impending court case. It was not so much the giving of evidence, but of what meeting Phil again might do to her. It was about eight months since she had last seen him and it had taken her most of that time to get herself together again. She had thought that at last she was over him, but now she wasn't all that sure. In spite of everything she couldn't find it in her heart to hate him. But it was no use agonising over the might-have-been. She would just have to be strong.

Impatient with her own indecision, she jumped out of bed, switched on the radio, bathed and breakfasted and finally relieved her pent-up feelings by going outside to give her blue Metro a much-needed wash.

Just as she was giving it a final polish, a man on a motorcycle sped up the lane and came to a halt outside the house next door. Removing his crash-helmet, he tucked it under his arm, gave Charlotte a pleasant 'good morning', walked up the path to the Cliftons' cottage and rang the bell.

'Excuse me,' she called to him, 'I don't think there's anyone in.'

'Oh—thanks.' He came back and perched on the low garden wall to talk to her. 'I phoned several times yesterday, but there was no reply. Are they away?'

The stranger seemed respectable enough —fortyish, polite, tidily dressed in a black weatherproof jacket—but something urged Charlotte to be careful. She had never seen him before and it wasn't her place to advertise Marjorie's whereabouts.

'I don't think so. Probably just out visiting,' she said. 'Can I take a message?'

'How long have you lived here?' he wanted to know, eyeing her curiously.

'About four months. Mrs Clifton and I are quite

good neighbours.'

The man gave a twisted smile. 'Well, I'm her husband. I daresay she's told you what a villain I am.'

Charlotte's mouth gaped a little. 'Well, no,' she said, 'we're not that close, just neighbourly. Why, are you a villain?' she added with a slow smile.

'Let's say I'm no plaster saint,' he admitted, 'but I love my little girl Debby and I want to see her. It's not right for the lass to suffer just because her mum and I fell out.'

'No-o,' Charlotte agreed thoughtfully, 'Debby's a nice kid. Anyway, I'll tell them you came. Does Marjorie know where to get in touch with you?'

'Yes, she knows. I'm working on the motorway—there's an office on the site—they'd get a message to me. That was the trouble really, us being separated, me not getting home as much as she wanted me to. There's a lot of weekend work, see, but it's a job. You have to go where the job is, don't you?'

'I suppose so.' Knowing the problems of unemployment in the area, Charlotte had to be sympathetic. She was almost tempted to tell him the truth, but she recalled Dr Challoner saying that Marjorie was adamant she did not want her husband told. Certainly an emotional upset was the last thing Marjorie needed in her present state. Yet surely the man had a right to see his child? 'I'll tell her you were asking,' she said.

'Thanks, love. No point in me hanging around here, I suppose. Tell her I'll be at me mam's until about eight tonight, if you see her before then.' He replaced his helmet and rode away on his motorcycle.

Gazing after him, Charlotte scratched her head in some concern. Had she done the right thing in keeping quiet—and what should she do now? Someone ought to be told that he'd been enquiring. Perhaps Robert would be the right person to consult since Marjorie was his patient. At least he could be relied upon for a level-headed approach to the problem. What the family reaction might be was another matter. The husband's explanation had sounded plausible, but that was only one side of the story.

Gathering up her cleaning materials, Charlotte went indoors and, with a certain amount of reluctance, dialled the doctor's home number. All that brought her was an answering machine giving an alternative emergency number or the invitation to leave a message. Which was a fat lot of use to her in the present situation, Charlotte despaired. Perhaps it would be best if she called in at the hospital herself that afternoon. Then she could see how Marjorie was and possibly have a word with the Ward Sister, or with the grandmother if she were visiting.

Sunday visiting at the Valley Community Hospital was from two-thirty to three-thirty. Timing her arrival somewhere in between, Charlotte found a dejected Debby standing in the doorway of the waiting-room outside Women's Medical, chewing a fingernail and watching other visitors coming and going.

'Hallo!' she greeted the little girl with a warm smile. 'How's your mummy—have you been in to see her yet?'

Debby's worried frown lifted at the sight of a

friend. She nodded. 'Yes—but only for a minute, because they don't allow children today, only Saturdays, and the Sister's ever so strict. I don't think me mam's much better, though.' Her little round face crumpled and she began to weep. 'I don't want her to die . . .'

A lump rose in Charlotte's own throat. She put her arms around the child and gave her a big hug. 'Cheer up, sweetheart, I'm sure it's not as bad as that. It always takes a little while for the medicine to make people better, you know.' Feeling in her jacket pocket for a tissue, she gently mopped up the little girl's tears. 'Who is with your mummy at the moment?'

'M-my gran and grandad.' Her chin wobbled piteously. 'I-I wish my daddy was here . . .'

'How long is it since you've seen him?' Charlotte prompted.

'I can't remember 'xactly. It was when he brought me an Easter egg. He didn't want to go away and leave us,' Debby added, her voice tremulous, 'but he had to, because of his work. Mam got cross with him—th-they shouted at each other.'

Charlotte sighed. 'Oh dear, that's a pity. But even grown-ups can't help quarrelling sometimes, pet.'

She was at a loss as to what else to say, not knowing how Marjorie was responding to treatment, or the precise nature of her illness for that matter. It would be totally wrong to assure Debby that all would be well if that were not the case. The best she could do was try to persuade someone to let the child have another few minutes with her mother.

'Well, you sit down here for a moment. You can look at one of those comics while and I go and have a little talk with Sister,' she said. 'I won't be long.' With a reassuring smile she went out into the corridor—and walked straight into Robert Challoner.

'Hallo!' His blue eyes switched beyond her to the small figure swinging her legs on a chair in the bare waiting-room. 'Still playing the guardian angel, are you?'

She was too thankful to see him to indulge in small talk. 'Oh Robert! Am I glad to see you!' Relief glowed in her welcoming smile. 'Have you got a moment?'

'Yes, what is it?' His perceptive gaze took in every nuance of her warm-hearted, animated features as she quickly explained the situation. What was it about this girl that got to him? She was a bundle of contradictions. He had watched her about the practice, where her pleasantness heartened everyone she met. She was extremely competent yet full of insecurities. He had seen her in the unguarded moment, feeling unloved and unwanted and needing to justify her existence. Which was a nonsense and made him want to thump whoever was responsible. She was also apt to creep into his thoughts in a most distracting fashion, a fact which made him respond testily now to the question she posed him.

Stoking his long nose, her retorted, 'Really, Charlotte, what am I supposed to do? I'm a doctor, not a marriage guidance counsellor.'

She tossed her fair head impatiently. 'Come on, it amounts to much the same thing. After all, it's people's personal problems that cause their health problems half the time. The thing is, should I have told Mr Clifton what was going on? I mean, I wondered whether it might be upsetting for her if he'd shown up here. How is she?'

'Quite poorly. She had a gastroscopy yesterday which showed a number of gastric bleeding points. No malignancy though, I'm glad to say. We hope it won't be necessary to operate.' He frowned thoughtfully, glancing along the corridor towards the open ward. 'I think she must be told—or perhaps the grandparents. It might even do some good. What was the husband like?'

Charlotte shrugged noncommittally. 'He *seemed* all right . . . your average middle-of-the-road sort of guy . . '

'Well, it's hardly my place to decide the issue. Let me have a word with Sister first,' Robert said, 'and then I'll go and see how the land lies.'

'Right, and while you're talking to Sister, could you persuade her to let Debby see her mum again?' Charlotte pleaded. 'The poor child's worried sick.'

'Why, what's stopping her seeing her mother?' The doctor threw a roguish wink in the youngster's direction.

'Saturday is children's day. Rules is rules! She was chucked out, apparently.'

Robert raised his eyes to heaven. 'Shades of Flo Nightingale! Leave it to me.'

Charlotte watched his leisurely, long-legged stride towards the Sister's office, saw him knock and enter and saw the Sister's angular features break into a welcoming smile as she rose to shake hands with him. Sister Horner was a large, raw-boned woman who had once been an Army nurse and brought military discipline to her well-run ward. Fair but firm was her reputation, but judging by that welcome, Charlotte felt confident that it wouldn't take Robert long to bend a few rules. She went back to sit and talk to Debby in an optimistic frame of mind.

They passed ten minutes playing noughts and crosses, during which time Charlotte discovered that Debby's paternal grandmother was a widow and lived at Ilkley. Which was near enough, by motorcycle at any rate, for her father to visit the hospital that evening, if it was felt desirable. Charlotte herself was highly glad to have passed on the responsibility for making that decision.

The bell for the end of afternoon visiting rang as Dr Challoner came back. Crooking his forefinger, he beckoned to Debby with a broad grin, and eagerly she slipped off her chair to join him. 'Don't you disappear,' he flung over his shoulder to Charlotte.

Gratified, she wandered out into the corridor to wait as, hand-in-hand, the big man and the small girl threaded their way through the departing visitors against the stream of the traffic.

Charlotte was joined in a few moments by the grandparents. 'We heard you was here, Nurse,' Mrs Dent said. 'It's real good of you to take so much trouble, lass. And good of the doctor, too, to let Debby see her mam again. That Sister's a bit of a tartar, isn't she?'

'Well, there are a lot of really ill people in medical wards,' Charlotte reasoned, 'so there do have to be rules, for everyone's sake. You've been told, I suppose, that Marjorie's husband called at their house?'

'Yes, and about time too!' Mr Dent returned.

Charlotte looked from one to the other. 'Was anything decided?'

'Oh, we'll give him a ring when we get home. Marjorie don't seem too bothered now, one way or t'other,' Mrs Dent went on.

'I'm glad of that. I do hate secrets, don't you? And Debby did tell me she wanted to see her dad,' Charlotte told them.

The grandmother let out a heavy sigh. 'Eee! I don't know—wedding vows bain't what they used to be in our young days. I blame the pill, meself . . .'

She would have carried on, but her husband cut her short, saying, 'Least said, soonest mended, Jean, and 'tis their own affair.'

'Yes, nothing much anyone else can do about it,' Charlotte agreed. 'Let's hope they can at least be friends, for Debby's sake. The most important thing at the moment is for Marjorie to get better.'

'She's a bit better than she was, thank God. But the doctor says she'll be here for a week or two, so we're going to move back to their house for the time being, because of Debby's schooling. Ah! Here she comes now . . .' Beaming, Mrs Dent held out a hand to her granddaughter whose chubby face was wreathed in smiles. 'All right now, duckie? Come on, let's go home and have some tea.'

Charlotte waved the little party on their way and

waited for Dr Challoner, as she had been asked. Coming from the ward in conversation with Sister Horner, Robert broke off to introduce her.

'Sister, do you know Miss Blythe, my practice nurse? She's especially interested in Mrs Clifton —they happen to be near neighbours.'

The Sister's smile was correct but impersonal as her grey eyes weighed up the younger girl. She passed no comment except to say that the ward was now closed and that she thought Mrs Clifton had really seen enough people for one afternoon.

'Yes, I'm sure she has,' Charlotte agreed, being equally professional. 'I only called in to deliver the message from her husband. Perhaps you'd be kind enough to give her my good wishes?'

After saying goodbye, doctor and nurse left together. They walked down the wide staircase to the ground floor. 'Did you manage to get everything sorted?' Charlotte asked.

'Yes, after a fashion. We've left it for the grandparents to get in touch with the husband and, if he wants to come, Mrs Clifton says she'll see him.' His mouth twisted wryly. 'My own instinct is that she'd like him to. I would guess she's still quite fond of him, whatever he may have done.'

Crossing the reception hall, they made for the main entrance and the car-park. The air outside was refreshingly wholesome after the confines of the hospital. A light breeze lifted the ends of Charlotte's hair and she breathed deeply and said: 'Mmm! What a lovely afternoon.'

They reached her car first, where he paused and turned to look at her. And there was absolutely no reason for her heart to go into arrhythmia when their eyes met and held, but it did. For one heart-stopping moment the world spun about her. Then he broke the spell by saying with a half-smile, 'And what are you going to do with the rest of it, Charlie?'

She looked away, searching in her shoulder bag for her car keys. 'Would you mind not calling me that?' she replied edgily.

'Why not? Is it a special privilege for the bouncy pharmacist?'

The veiled irony in his tone made her angry. 'No,' she flashed, 'it's unfeminine. I don't like it.'

'Ah! Point taken,' he returned with bland good humour. 'Still, there's no sense in getting paranoid about it. And you haven't answered my first question.'

His concentrated gaze was beginning to unnerve her, sparking off sensual reactions which she had to fight against. 'I've forgotten what it was,' she declared, deliberately offhand, unsmiling.

Robert's dark brows contracted. 'I merely asked what you were going to be doing with the rest of the day. You appear to be in a negative sort of mood, though, so you'll probably tell me it's none of my business. Forget it.' He made an airy gesture. 'Goodbye, Charlotte.' Thrusting his hands into his trouser pockets, he stalked off towards his own car, displeasure evident in every inch of his rugged frame.

'Hell!' she muttered, mad with herself for over-reacting and even madder with him for his lofty rejoinder. What right had he to get shirty just because she objected to the boyish nickname?

Inwardly, though, Charlotte was aware that there had been more to it than a skirmish over a name. Ridiculous though it was, her flare-up had been a kind of self-defence against his powerful appeal to her senses. But she should be able to control her feelings without wrecking the peace, for goodness' sake!

And suppose she had told him that she was doing nothing special for the rest of the day, what then? Was he about to suggest doing something together? Well, she had certainly nipped *that* in the bud, Charlotte thought wryly. All for the best, perhaps. In any case, she was probably making a great drama out of nothing. He probably hadn't given her another thought once they parted company.

Had she known it, nothing could have been further from the truth. Robert Challoner was kicking himself for being an insensitive fool, now he thought about it. So she had a chip on her shoulder about being called Charlie? Maybe she was entitled and knowing why, he should have been more understanding. His medical training ought to have given him *some* insight into human frailties. More so than that chap Bryan she'd been with at the barbecue. A decent enough sort of fellow no doubt, but hardly her type. He wondered whether the pharmacist also had been put firmly in his place for using the nickname. It gave him a certain amount of satisfaction to think so.

Manoeuvring past him on the way out of the car-park, Charlotte gave the doctor a toot and wave, as a kind of gesture of goodwill.

Obviously not one for bearing grudges, he was

relieved to note. A quick burst of temper now and then, but all over in five minutes. He resolved to be more tactful in his future dealings with her, because she was a nice kid. Bright, too. *Kid?* Who was he trying to fool? The girl was a lovely, desirable woman—a Lorelei—and he had best be aware of that.

CHAPTER FIVE

MONDAY morning saw Charlotte back in the familiar atmosphere of the Health Centre, where her work kept her fully engrossed for most of the time. There was no doubt that since Robert's arrival a new vigour had swept through the whole establishment, with everyone keen to provide a really good service for the patients. There was something about the man which boosted morale. Even Mrs Clench, their cleaner, with a perpetual air of aggrievance on account of her haemorrhoids, was won over by him.

'He's all right, is Dr Challoner,' she confided to Charlotte, taking her a mid-morning mug of coffee between patients. 'Took a real interest in my haemmydreds. He's sending me to a specialist to get something done about 'em.' Mrs Clench hitched her girdle down to a more comfortable position and allowed herself the luxury of a smile. 'So I forgive 'im for missing the waste-bin every time he chucks something at it. Not the tidiest chap in the world. I told him straight, he oughter find himself a good wife.'

'And what did he say to that?' Charlotte asked, mildy curious.

'Oh, just laughed and said he's far too busy to go courtin'. But he wouldn't have no trouble if he wanted to, I reckon. There's some here as wouldn't need asking twice,'' the cleaner said meaningfully, nodding her head in the general direction of Wendy Fenner's surgery.

The communicating door to Robert's office opened at that moment and he looked in. 'Excuse me, Charlotte, I need some more KY jelly . . . when you've a moment. Finish your drink.' He flung a brief smile in the cleaner's direction and disappeared again behind his own door.

'Eeee!' sighed Mrs Clench, shaking her head, 'If only me old man were that 'andsome!'

'It's not always the good-lookers who make the best husbands,' Charlotte smiled, swallowing the last of her coffee.

'Aye, you're right there, lass,' the other agreed, and picking up the empty mug she went on her way.

Charlotte went to her neat and tidy cupboard in the small dispensary, which she had reduced from a fair degree of past chaos to its present orderly state. She was responsible for stocks and making sure they were never out of supplies. It was easy to find the tube of lubricant, and she knocked and took it in to the doctor.

She found him alone, writing up the notes on his last patient. As yet she'd had no chance to say anything to anyone about her forthcoming appearance as a witness, and it struck her that now was as good a time as any.

'Thanks,' he said, glancing up when she put the tube on his desk. Laying down his pen, he balled a spoiled presciption sheet, swivelled in his chair and aimed the paper at his metal waste-bin. It landed on the floor.

Charlotte crossed to pick up the wayward missile, along with a few other strays. 'Mrs Clench said you were a rotten shot,' she remarked.

Robert curbed a smile and fixed her with a penetrating gaze from under his dark brows. 'I wondered why my ears were burning.'

She couldn't help noticing how deeply blue his eyes were, enhanced by the deep blue shirt he was wearing. 'She forgives you only because you're going to do something about her *haemmydreds,*' Charlotte reported.

'Poor Mrs Clench. I thought it was time somebody did.'

He seemed to be in an agreeable frame of mind, and so she went on quickly, 'Actually, while I'm here, Robert, I ought to tell you that I have to take the day off on Friday.'

His analytical gaze seemed to be taking her apart inch by inch and she felt her cheeks getting pinker by the minute. 'Nothing wrong, I hope?' he asked quietly.

'No, at least, I hope not.' She passed a tongue over dry lips and went on to explain about the court case, feeling already like a prisoner in the dock under the impact of his scrutiny.

'Ah, I see. Well, there should be nothing to worry about from your point of view.' He flexed his broad shoulders, leaned back lazily in his chair and clasped his hands behind the classic curve of his dark head. 'Just tell it like it was, and don't let the prosecution trick you into passing a medical opinion, which of course you shouldn't do . . .'

He broke off as Helen, the receptionist, knocked and came in with another batch of patients' notes. 'Quite a few people waiting, doctor, and for you, Charlotte,' Helen said briskly, and departed with a look of mild reproach.

Robert checked his wrist-watch and made a mournful face. 'I never seem to have the time to talk to you properly. There are a number of things I'd like to discuss. Are you free tonight?'

'Er, yes,' she returned, wondering what things in particular he had in mind. Working lunches with various members of the primary health care team normally took place on a Friday in the staff room, although there was invarably someone missing. This time it would be herself.

'Fine,' he said. 'Let's have a working dinner—say after evening surgery? I should be through by seven.'

That agreed, they both got back to work.

Charlotte's last patient before lunch was a Mr Terry Street, referred to her by Dr Mac for an electrocardiograph. He was a stocky man of thirty-five and, reading his notes, Charlotte saw he was a heavy drinker and smoker. His occupation was given as a turf accountant.

Dressed in a trendy check suit and sporting enough gold jewellery to impress an oil-rich sheik, he swaggered into her office, raised his sandy eyebrows and stuck out a large hand to shake hers. 'Hallo, sweetheart. Where've they been hiding you, then? I'd have come a bit sooner if I'd known you were on the menu.'

She smiled, liking the big, butch fellow in spite of

his brashness. 'Hallo, Mr Sweet. Dr McAllister wants you to have an ECG—you've been having some chest pains, is that right?'

'Yes, love. Indigestion I reckon, but my girlfriend said I ought to have a health check since my old man had a dicky heart. You know what women are, born worriers.'

Charlotte sensed a degree of anxiety beneath his show of nonchalance, but she laughed softly and said, 'You should take it as a compliment that she doesn't want to lose you.'

'Yeah . . . or could be she doesn't want to lose a meal ticket. What do I have to take off, everything?'

'No, not quite down to basics. Just your jacket and shirt and shoes and socks, and then if you'll get up on the table, Mr Street . . .' She wheeled the ECG machine into position and plugged in the main cable.

'The name's Terry,' he breezed, slipping off his jacket and tie, 'What's yours?'

'Charlotte.' She eyed his hairy chest as he pulled up his shirt and unbuttoned it. 'I shall have to shave some of that hair off, I'm afraid, or the terminals won't stick.'

'OK, sweetheart, spoil my manly charm if you must!' He kept up a flow of cheerful chatter while she prepared the sites and attached the electrodes to the specific pulse points.

Switching on the machine, Charlotte watched the tracing as it was recorded. At first glance she could see no startling deviation from normal, but something about the pattern worried her a little.

'That seems all right,' she told him quietly, detaching the terminals. 'You can get dressed again now.''

Sitting up, Terry peered over her shoulder at the peaks and troughs of his cardiac cycle. 'Can you make head or tail out of that? Goes up and down a lot, doesn't it?'

'You'd be in real trouble if it didn't!' she reasurred him. 'Actually I'm not an expert at reading these things. I'll let Dr McAllister have it while you're getting dressed. You're going back to see him, are you?'

'Well, no. He had to go out in a hurry while I was waiting for you, but he said as you'd show it to someone else of there was owt wrong.'

'Oh. Did he say anything to you about cutting down on the drinks and smokes?'

'Yeah,' Terry returned lightly, 'told me I ought to watch it. Said my blood pressure was up a bit.'

Charlotte was still studying the tracing, not altogether happy with the result. 'He wasn't just saying it for fun, you know,' she said. 'Your chest pains could have been a timely warning.'

He replaced his shirt and knotted his tie about his thick neck, giving her a saucy grin. 'Tell you what, have a weekend away with me and I promise I'll give it a go.'

She rolled her eyes in mock despair. 'Goodbye, Terry.'

'No? Pity,' he chuckled, and bent down to put on his shoes and socks. Almost immediately, he straightened up again, holding his midriff and taking a quick sharp breath. 'Bloody—indigestion again . . .'

Charlotte's alert green eyes took in his stricken expression and the bluish tinge which had crept around his nose and lips. Pushing forward a chair, she hid her concern by saying calmly, 'Sit down for a moment until it goes off . . . don't hurry.'

She was scared that a heart attack might be imminent and decided someone else ought to take a look at him there and then. The nearest person was Robert. Tapping on their dividing door, she found him clearing his desk before leaving.

'Can you spare me a moment, please?' She put the ECG tracing on the desk in from of him. 'I've just recorded this. It's a Mr Street, one of Mac's patients, but Mac had to go out in a hurry. The S-T segment looked a bit raised—and Mr Street has just had a sharp, stabbing pain. Would you see him?''

With resigned patience the doctor studied the tracing, reopened his medical case and took out his stethoscope. 'Got his notes?'

'Yes, on my desk.' Charlotte followed after him as he made for the treatment room and greeted the patient.

'Hallo, Mr Sweet. I'm Dr Challoner. You're not feeling too good, I hear,' he said, reaching for the patient's radial pulse.

Terry smoothed his free hand over his sweaty face and agreed, yes, he did have a bit of a turn, but he was OK now, he thought. 'No need to bother you, Doc.'

Robert went to check on the notes. 'I'll be the judge of that. How did you come here?'

'By car. Got the Merc outside.'

Unbuttoning the patient's shirt, the doctor slipped his stethoscope into position and listened to the heart sounds. After a few moment he folded up the instrument and stuffed it in his pocket, saying decisively, 'Well my friend you'll not be doing any more driving for a week or two. I want you to leave your car keys with Nurse. I'm on my way to the hospital now. I'll take you there myself—we'll get you admitted as an emergency.'

The big bookmaker's eyes widened. 'You saying I *have* got a heart problem?'

'I'm afraid so, and in need of prompt attention. In hospital they'll be better able to make a correct diagnosis and decide on the right course of action. It may be only rest you need, combined with the appropriate medication.'

'B-but . . . I can't drop everything . . . just like that!'

Robert minced no words. 'If you don't, you might be forced to drop everything, *permanently*, just like that!' he warned.

Terry gave a defeated shrug, reluctantly fished his keys out of his trouser pocket and handed them over to Charlotte. He managed a feeble grin. 'I started to have palpitations soon as I looked at you,' he cracked. 'Nurses as pretty as her should come with a health warning, eh, Doc?'

'We've had no complaints so far,' Robert returned with a wry smile, seeing the colour flood her cheeks. 'Come through to my office when you're ready, Mr Street.' He went back to his own room to get his things together.

Charlotte helped her patient on with his jacket. 'I'm glad he's taking you in,' she said soothingly. 'It may be only for a short while, but it's best to have a thorough check-up, isn't it?'

He looked despondent. 'Bloody 'ell! Me girlfriend'll go spare. She flaps if I'm five minutes late home . . .'

'Oh, you'll be surprised. Sometimes it takes a crisis to bring out the best in people. Would you like me to get in touch with her, or anyone?'

'Please. Hilary don't drive . . . but my mate Steve can collect the car.' Fishing in his breast pocket, he found a business card and gave it to her. 'If you'll . . . ring this number, they'll do the necessary. And thanks, lass, you're a winner,' he added between laboured breaths.

She wished him good luck as, ponderously, he went through to the doctor's surgery. Then she made the requested telephone call, giving a brief explanation without being alarmist. 'I'll leave the car keys with our receptionist,' she said, 'there's always somebody here until seven o'clock.'

Tidying up her treatment room ready for the afternoon baby clinic, she fell to brooding on the unpredictable. However in control of your life you thought you were, there was no telling what a capricious fate might have in store for you.

Her clinic not starting until three, Charlotte had time to go home for lunch. The post had arrived in her absence—the promised letter from the solicitor giving her the venue for the hearing and asking her to meet him there at ten a.m. on the Friday. Altogether the journey would take her about four hours, she reckoned, what with having to change trains at York and going on from King's Cross to the Law Courts, so it would be best to travel down the night before.

As she had already fixed to stay at Amy's flat, that was no problem, but not knowing how long the court case would take was going to alter her weekend plans yet again. Once more she would have to put off her visit home, and she rang the farm to explain why.

It was her father's housekeeper, Mrs Woods, who answered her call. 'Oh, you've just missed your dad, my love,' she said, 'he's gone over to Kettleby to see someone.'

'Kettleby? What's so fascinating about Kettleby these days?' Charlotte asked. 'That's where he'd gone last time I rang.'

Mrs Woods went on, 'Well, your dad met Mrs Rymer at an antiques sale a while ago. She was selling a few bits of furniture as her son had got married and brought his bride to live at the farm, and naturally they wanted some modern stuff of their own. Your dad was after a grandfather clock, which he didn't get, and Mrs Rymer told him about this clock she had at home and couldn't bear to part with although it didn't work, and your dad's been going over there trying to fix if for her.'

'Hmmm . . . ' Charlotte murmured, 'sounds very interesting! What d'you reckon, Woody? Anything cooking?'

The housekeeper chuckled. 'We-ell, he did say as how he's always wanted a grandfather clock, and the one she's got is a gem. I don't know about the lady, but she invited him to dinner and he took her a box o' chocolates. And he's kind of perky these days. Would you mind if he's found himself a girlfriend?'

'Mind? I'd be really chuffed,' Charlotte enthused. 'I don't like the idea of him spending a lonely old age. And if she shares his passion for clocks, she's off to a good start, isn't she?'

'Now, now,' warned Mrs Woods,' don't you go putting two and two together—might come to nowt. And don't you let on I said anything, or he'll think I'm a gossip.'

'OK, I'll be discretion itself,' Charlotte promised. 'If there's anything to tell, I expect he'll tell me when he wants to.'

After giving the housekeeper the details of her obligatory trip to London, Charlotte rang off feeling pleasantly intrigued about her father's movements. She hoped something good would come of it. Even if it didn't go beyond friendship, that was not to be despised. In Aunt Hannah's day such goings on would definitely have been discouraged.

Thinking ahead to her 'working dinner' with Robert, Charlotte packed a change of clothes before going back to the Health Centre that afternoon. She had no idea where they would go to eat, but she would certainly feel more at ease knowing that she looked presentable. She decided on a slim white linen dress and navy jacket, smart but not over-dressy.

He had been extremely nice to her today, for no apparent reason than that they had worked well together. Perhaps that little contretemps in the car-park yesterday was really nothing personal. Perhaps something or someone else had put him out and she had happened to be a handy target. Was he now trying to make amends? *Fat chance*! she told herself, more likely it was a favour he wanted. All the same, in spite of being a little apprehensive she was pleased he had asked her.

Back at the Health Centre, as usual, her work claimed her full attention. Babies and toddlers for immunisation were duly injected, and admired, and their progress noted, and their problems were discussed. The supply of sweeties with which she rewarded toddlers all but gave out.

There were no insoluble problems on the whole, but the tail-end of the afternoon brought a case which saddened her. Tammy Briggs, a baby girl of three months, was presented for her first dose of triple vaccine—a poor little scrap with a runny nose and a severe nappy rash—and she was brought in not by her unmarried schoolgirl mother, but by the girl's aunt.

'She never ought to have had the bairn, Nurse, really she shouldn't,' the well-meaning aunt complained. 'But there you are, it was against their religion to do owt about it. And now she's got her she don't seem to care for her, poor wee thing. And her own mum's not much help . . . suffers with her nerves, and no wonder! They moved house a couple of months back. Nobody's looked at the baby since then, so perhaps you'd give her the once-over, would you, love?'

'Yes, of course.' Charlotte took the mewling, rather whiffy infant and undressed and examined her gently. She looked for marks of abuse on the little body, but there were none. The baby appeared to be fairly well nourished if slightly underweight. Her rectal temperature was correct, her reflexes normal, her blue eyes were responsive and her fontanelle closed. But she had the sorest bottom that Charlotte had ever seen. It was amazing how babies could thrive even in adverse circumstances, Charlotte marvelled.

'Dear me!' she said. 'What have they been washing her nappies in?'

'Search me!' the aunt returned. 'Stiff as a board some of 'em are. Reckon they just dry off the wet ones. And there's some women as 'ld give anything to have a bairn and care for it. Rum old world isn't it?'

'It is indeed!' Charlotte agreed. She bathed the baby's buttocks and applied some soothing antiseptic cream before putting on a disposable nappy, of which she kept a small supply for such emergencies. She cleansed the messy little button nose while making comforting noises to her small patient, 'There, that's better, isn't it?' Charlotte cooed. Returning Tammy to the aunt's arms, she went on, 'Do you live near the family?'

'No, I was just visiting, but I offered to bring her for her injection. My sister-in-law's got a migraine and my niece is at school . . . but they do want it done.'

'We-ell, I think we should leave that for today—wait until her cold's better. Just a moment, I'll confirm with the doctor . . .'

The doctor in attendance was Wendy and she was locking her desk prior to leaving when Charlotte came to seek her advice. She frowned, casting her mind back as the situation was explained to her. 'Yes, I remember a Mrs Briggs coming to register—she wanted some tranquillisers—but I didn't tie her up with a teenage daughter and a baby. Why hasn't any health visitor called?'

Charlotte shrugged. 'This one slipped through the net, I suppose, on account of the move.'

'Do you want me to take a look at her now,' Wendy asked, 'or are you happy about her?'

'If one can be *happy* about an unwanted baby,' Charlotte said with a rueful smile. 'Physically it's just a sore bott and a runny nose, but do you agree the triple vaccine should be postponed until she's in better shape?'

'Yes, yes ... and I'll get her on to Ruth's caseload so that she doesn't get overlooked in future. Anything else?'

Wendy was obviously in a hurry to be somewhere else and reluctant to be dealing with grubby infants, but Charlotte was not to be rushed. 'Will you write her an EC10 for some Sudocrem and some cold medicine? Pity you can't order a supply of mother love as well,' she added while the doctor wrote the prescription.

'If only we could!' Wendy sighed. 'If only we could!'

Back in her treatment room Charlotte handed over the prescription form. 'This is for some cream for her nappy rash and some mixture for her cold—half a teaspoonful three times a day. And Dr Fenner agrees we should leave the injection for this week. The health visitor will be calling, but tell the family not to hesitate to get in touch if they're at all worried.' She smiled at the aunt. 'Good of you to help out. Goodbye.'

Preening herself that she at least had done the right thing, the aunt departed with her small niece, promising to call at the chemist on the way home.

Charlotte made her own notes on the baby's record card and went to the staff room for a quick cup of tea before evening surgery began. Through the window she saw Robert's BMW turn in at the Health Centre car-park. She watched him ease his long legs from the driving seat and admired his muscular thighs as he leaned to reach inside for his medical bag before locking the car door. She saw Wendy, on her way out, pause for a brief word before getting into her own car. Robert's arm went round her shoulders in an affectionate hug and Charlotte felt a stab of what could only be described as envy.

Ruth, the health visitor, came into the staff room just then, all bright and breezy. 'Hallo!' she said. 'What's up with you? Bad day?'

'Not really,' Charlotte smiled, dismissing her private thoughts, 'just busy. Got a new job for you, though. I'd better give you the details in case Wendy hasn't left a note.'

She proceeded to tell Ruth all about Baby Briggs and the health visitor raised her eyebrows despairingly. 'Oh dear! Another misguided youngster. Well, I'll do what I can . . .'

The telephone lines had been switched over and the rest of the staff had left before Robert had finished with his last patient that evening. Charlotte had washed and changed and was sorting through some drug companies' literature while waiting for him.

'Oh, there you are,' he said, coming through to her office to find her. 'Ready?'

'Yes, ready and waiting. I was beginning to think you'd forgotten me!' she joked.

He ran an appreciative eye over her lissom figure in the slim white dress. 'I may get absorbed in my work, but not to the total exclusion of life's lighter moments, I can assure you.'

'Oh? I thought this was to be a 'working dinner'?'

As he watched her, his lips twitched. 'Put away your little whip, Charlotte. We may touch on work later, but at the moment I'm finding the view too distracting. Shall we go?' He lifted her navy jacket from the back of the chair and held it out for her to slip into, letting his hands rest lightly on her shoulders for an instant.

The brief physical contact sent a ripple of pleasure though her blood. His powerful body so close behind her filled her with a sense of urgency. She was only too well aware that had his arms slid around her she could not have fought against her natural desire. That innate charm of his was working well. Oh heavens! This was sheer stupidity. She must pull herself together. Picking up her shoulder-bag, she led the way along the corridor and out into the car-park. 'Where to?' she said. 'Shall I follow you in my car?'

'Indeed you will not!' He unlocked the BMW. 'I'll bring you back to pick yours up. Hop in.'

Meekly she did so, stealing a glance at his carefree expression as he slipped smoothly into gear and drove off.

'Hope you're hungry,' he went on. 'I thought I'd spoil you tonight. Don't ask me why . . . probably due to the rising sap or something.'

This playful side of him was new to her and she laughed softly. 'I'll settle for the *or something*. We'll leave the rising sap in its proper place, I think.'

He grinned and concentrated on navigating through the High Street traffic until they were out on to the open road. 'Mr Street's Mercedes has gone, I noticed,' he remarked.

'Yes, his partner collected the keys from Helen this afternoon. He didn't have any more trouble on the way to the hospital, I assume?'

'No . . . he was a bit agitated, but we got him there in one piece and they put him to bed. Crescendo angina, predisposing to an MI, I imagine. Good thinking on your part querying that ECG,' Robert allowed.

'I do have my inspired moments. Oh, is that why I'm getting spoiled tonight?'

'Uh-uh!' He shook his head. 'Just thought it would do us both good, seeing that we've had our noses to the grindstone lately. And I'm not on call tonight.' The sleek car flew steadily on through the hilly moorland countryside with the tranquil evening sky growing pink and grey like a dove's wing. 'Much better driving out a bit than staying in town, don't you think?'

The serenity around them was in sharp contrast to her own uncertain state of mind. She was not at all sure as to the wisdom of this trip, knowing his power to arouse her primal instincts, but she nodded. 'Yes, much better . . .' Then she frowned. 'This route seems vaguely familiar . . .'

'I daresay it is. I've booked a table at Friars Court—where Dr Bates had her retirement party, remember?'

As if she would ever forget! That night seemed to have been the catalyst which had reawakened the old nightmare days for Charlotte. And it had underlined her own vulnerability. She was still capable of being bowled over by a hunk of masculinity with a pair of gorgeous blue eyes, fool that she was. She fell silent, wondering where she was heading and what the coming Friday held in store.

Robert gave her a cryptic sideways look. 'Well, I didn't expect a round of applause,' he said ironically. 'I know it's where Lynne broke her wrist, but you can't hold that against the place!'

Charlotte laughed. 'Sorry, I was thinking of something else, that's all. I'm impressed, honestly. Have you been here since the party?'

They had entered the sweeping gravelled drive leading to the floodlit country hotel.

'Yes, a couple of times,' Robert said, not elaborating, but it did not escape Charlotte that the *maître d'hôtel*—when he brought menus to them in the cocktail bar—knew Dr Challoner well enough to greet him cordially by name.

The gracious oak-beamed restuarant had an intimate atmosphere with its red candles glowing in glass globes on the crisp white tablecloths, and everywhere the gleam of well-polished silver. It was a popular eating-place for both holidaymakers and locals, but Charlotte and Robert were shown to a secluded alcove table with the minimum of delay. Although there was a full and exotic bill of fare, they had both opted for the speciality of the house, the succulent roast baron of beef which sat in pride of place on an enormous covered silver platter.

'. . . and if you've got room for desert afterwards, Wendy goes a bundle on the *crêpes Suzette* here,' Robert told her.

Flattered though she was by his attentions, the mention of Wendy's name brought Charlotte down to earth with a bump. So it was Wendy he brought here as a rule. She thought she had better guide conversation to the real purpose of this meeting. 'What was it you particularly wanted to talk about?' she said.

He made a comic face. 'Determined to ruin my digestion, are you?'

Charlotte laughed. 'It was your idea to talk about work, and our days are pretty full, so perhaps we ought to make the most of it. Especially since I'll be away this Friday . . .' She broke off while they were served with their meal.

'How long do you think you'll be away?' Robert asked, the full force of his lively blue eyes meeting hers across the table.

She shrugged and lowered her lashes as she helped herself to horseradish sauce. 'It depends, I suppose, if they think there's a case to answer. I *hope* I'll be back in time for work on the Monday.'

'Tell me about what happened . . . I know one has to be so careful these days. Litigation is getting almost as bad here as it is in America.'

Charlotte gave him the bare facts of the incident

and admitted that she was a little worried about having to appear as a witness. 'Phil—er—Dr Erskine really did do a good job on this man, and it was definitely the man's own choice to go home. He wasn't confused or mentally disturbed. Apart from his ripe language he seemed rational. The trouble was, he shot off before we could get his signature on a self-discharge form.'

'Pity. Nothing much you could do about that, then.' Robert eyed her between her narrowed brows. 'This Dr Erskine, would that be the chap who took you for a ride?'

It must have been a shot in the dark, but it didn't occur to her to deny it. 'Yes, as a matter of fact, it is. I wish I didn't have to go,' she added, feeling her colour rise, 'but I don't have any choice in the matter, and in any case I couldn't bear to see him blamed for what wasn't his fault.'

'No . . . that's not your style. Is it the thought of meeting him again that worries you? How do you feel about him these days?' Robert asked in the same tone of voice that he might use to a troubled patient.

'A bit embarrassed about the whole thing really,' Charlotte confessed. 'I don't hate him, if that's what you mean. He's a likeable guy, honestly, or I wouldn't have liked him, would I? Perhaps it's me that's not lovable or he wouldn't have let me go,' she said, half to herself.

'Don't talk rot, and stop putting yourself down!' he returned firmly. 'You should thank your lucky stars you're well out of it. Same as I do.'

She glanced across at him, her eyes rounding in surprise. 'What do you mean by that?'

He finished his meal and put his knife and fork carefully together, suppressing a smile. 'You're not the only one with a past, you know. 'D'you fancy that *crêpe*?'

'No thanks, I'm full.'

'Too bad!' he sighed. 'Wendy is putty in my hands for one of those!'

'Sorry to disappoint you,' Charlotte replied in the same bantering manner.

'Right, we'll have coffee in the lounge and I'll tell you the story of my life, shall I?'

'Well that would make a change from talking about me,' she agreed. 'You never did tell me why you really decided to swap computers for medicine.'

CHAPTER SIX

CHARLOTTE felt relaxed and easy with Robert in his present outgoing mood. They sat side by side in the cushioned comfort of the attractive lounge bar, and she sipped her creamy Irish coffee as near utterly content as she had been for a long time.

The furnishings were cottage-style, the floral linen loose covers over the upholstery matching the curtains at the mullion-paned windows, and there were prints of well-known Yorkshire beauty spots on the walls. An imitation log fire glowed in the ancient stone fireplace, all adding to that sense of well-being. And whether it was her potent drink or her companion's friendliness that was resonsible for her state of bliss Charlotte was not inclined to analyse. It was sufficient that he was there, within touching distance, and they were in mutual harmony.

Over the rim of her glass she caught the doctor's eye and they smiled at each other.

'You . . .' he observed with a touch of whimsy, 'look like a very contented cat. If I stroked you I think you might start purring.'

'My name is Charlotte, not Wendy,' she returned, matching his manner.

'Whoops! I *was* joking when I said that about Wendy,' he hastened to explain. 'It wasn't a character assassination. The trouble with me is my jokes sometimes tend to misfire.'

Charlotte waved a careless hand. 'Don't worry about it. I understand—you're just good friends! Have you known each other long? I mean, before you joined the practice?' she was bold enough to ask.

'Not really. Not in that sense, although I did meet her professionally a couple of years ago.' Robert became more serious for a moment. 'It was when I was a casualty officer in the Midlands. Her brother was brought to us after an accident and I had to break the news that he had died.'

'Oh, I see.' Charlotte's lambent green eyes were sympathetic. 'What was it . . . a road accident?'

'The result of one. There were complicating factors. Anyway, I was as surprised to meet up with her again here as I was to bump into you.' Changing the subject, he went on cheerfully, 'And how's your dad?'

'All bright-eyed and bushy-tailed, so I'm led to believe by our daily help. I haven't seen him lately, but she thinks he may be courting.'

Robert grinned and glanced pointedly around the lounge at a number of couples in various states of togetherness. 'There's a lot of it going on. What did I tell you about the rising sap?'

'You also said you were going to tell me about your own murky past,' she prompted.

'So I did, although that's probably another goof on my part. Actually it's not that interesting,' he went on. 'Umpteen other people could tell you a similar saga.'

'Very likely. The same as umpteen other girls like me have come unstuck with a married man.'

Robert let his discerning eyes rove steadily over the desirable young woman sitting beside him, and his thoughts went back to that other desirable woman he had married fourteen years ago. 'Ye-es, well, it happened to me in reverse,' he told her wryly. 'We'd been married for just over two years when my wife ran off with her ex-boss, and took our baby daughter with her.'

Charlotte's bright eyes clouded with dismay. 'Oh gosh! Sorry . . . I-I didn't mean to . . . ' she began lamely. 'Don't tell me if you'd rather not.'

He shrugged his broad shoulders philosophically. 'It's a long time ago now, and I eventually came to terms. Bearing grudges does nobody any good—I found that out the hard way. I know it sounds trite, Charlotte, but time does heal. Or at least, distance drops a convenient curtain.'

She couldn't imagine how any girl in her right senses could walk out on someone like Robert. True, he was a dominant personality and could be awkward. On the whole though he was approachable and good-humoured. In spite of being tough, he could be surprisingly gentle and understanding. All that, plus a stunning physique and that elusive something which could make your stomach flip when he looked at you! (At least, it did Charlotte's.) Where did his marriage go wrong?

As though divining her thoughts, he told her: 'We were far too young. We both had volatile tempers. We hadn't a clue about give and take. And he was established—he had more money than I did.'

There was a trace of rancour in his voice which made her long to take him in her arms and comfort him although his pain was in the past. 'What about the baby?' she ventured. 'Was there a legal battle?'

'Good lord, no. I did have that much sense. Jane was a good mother. She just happened to fall out of love with me. My daughter's twelve now. I have access, and a civilised relationship with my ex-wife. That's why I was going to Canada that time when I first met you. They live near Toronto. Sharon has two stepbrothers and she seems perfectly happy. They all treat me like an absentee uncle.' He paused. 'If she wants to come to me ever, then naturally I'll be glad to have her.'

'But . . . how can you be so reasonable about it!' Charlotte cried. 'That was far worse than what happened to me—and that was bad enough.'

He glanced at her with a sideways grin. 'Reasonable . . . me? Does that mean I've got the seal of approval in spite of everything?'

Charlotte felt her cheeks grow hot. 'Well, it wasn't you who did the walking out, was it?'

'No, but I might've driven Jane to it. I had a pretty short fuse in those days. I was raving when it first happened.' He propped his scarred shin across his other thigh and rubbed it thoughtfully. 'That's when I took myself off to Ben Nevis, to pit my rage against the elements. Perhaps subconciously my accident was retaliation. I remember thinking as I fell—now she'll be sorry! What I succeeded in doing was smashing my leg and landing in hospital for six months. And she didn't come near me. And that, Miss Blythe, is how the wonderful world of computers lost one of its brilliant sons.'

'And so modest with it!' Charlotte joked. 'But I don't really see the connection. You don't write programmes with your legs, do you?'

He shook his dark head. 'You miss the point. All those dedicated doctors and sweet young nurses flitting round, bullying me to pull my fainthearted self together . . . what could I do but join the ranks and repay my debt? So you see, we all fail sometimes. And you're not going to go into a decline, are you, just because you'll be seeing Jack-the-lad again? Give him one of your bewitching smiles and let him see he didn't even dent your ego.'

'Yes, Robert,' she said dutifully.

'. . . and as I said, thank your stars you had a lucky escape, even if it did hurt at the time.'

'Yes, Robert,' she said again.

He reached out to flick the ends of her lustrous fair hair. 'You can cut out that butter-wouldn't-melt stuff,' he returned mildly. 'Save it for the witness box.'

A bubble of laughter rose in her throat. 'Yes Robert,' she repeated.

He tutted. 'Enough of this insubordination or I shall be forced to take corrective measures. Come on, time I took you home.'

Outside, the pink and grey sky had gone, to be replaced by a black star-studded vault with a full moom silvering the countryside. It was a pleasing ride back to the Health Centre. Could have been very romantic, she thought, if you happened to be in love. As things were, they did at last get round to matters concerning the practice.

'I was dicussing German measles with Mac,' Robert told her. 'We decided on a check-search through the records to make sure that all the ten-year-old girls get notified they should come for immunisation. We had a young primigravida who hadn't been. Luckily she was past the danger time when she contracted it. Once we get our computer installed any amount of data will be there at the touch of a button, which will assist keeping tracks.'

'So your computer training will come in handy after all,' Charlotte said. 'But you're not going in for computerised consultations, are you? That's too cold-blooded.'

The doctor smiled. 'No, we won't be going that far. We realise the personal touch may be as useful as any pills we can prescibe. Some hospitals are experimenting with computers to confirm diagnoses, but they have to be fed with the correct information in the first place, so it still boils down to eyes, ears and asking the right questions to begin with.'

He also went on to tell her about the Good Health Day which the local health council planned to put on at the parish hall. 'There'll be films on a number of related topics and experts to counsel on everything from birth to bereavement. We've been asked to lend our support. Can we volunteer your services for a couple of hours on women's problems?'

'Mmm. Glad to,' agreed Charlotte. 'I suppose lots of people would be prepared to go to something like that whereas they might put off seeking advice otherwise.'

Wendy's white Renault was sitting in the car-park when they arrived back at the Health Centre, and there was a light within her surgery area. It was gone eleven. Robert frowned. 'What's she doing here?'

'Forgotten something, perhaps?' said Charlotte.

'I'd better see that everything's all right . . .' He was making for the back entrance when the lights in the surgery went out and the next moment Dr Fenner emerged. Wearing a green safari-style jacket and skirt, she looked, as ever, poised and stylish.

She paused in surprise on seeing the two of them. 'Hallo, Bob! Charlotte . . . I wondered why your car was still here.' Glancing from one to the other, she enquired with interest, 'What have you two been up to . . . or shouldn't I ask?'

'We might ask you the same thing,' Robert returned with a puckered smile. 'Problems?'

'Me? Oh, nothing earth-shaking. Just checking up on something for my own peace of mind. I had to make a night call to a toddler. His mother's in hospital with a new baby and his dad was in a flap because the child had a troublesome cough. Anyway, I did what I could and reassured dad that it was just a chill and that junior wasn't about to peg out. Then, after I'd left, *I* started worrying. I mean, all sorts of things begin with cold symptoms, don't they? So I came in to check on the lad's history, and to make sure he'd had all the right protective cover, which he had, thank goodness.'

Wendy crossed herself and wiped imaginary sweat from her porcelain brow. 'Children!' she sighed, 'they terrify me! Give me geriatrics any day.'

Charlotte laughed. 'This afternoon I gathered that you weren't too keen on the little dears.'

'Oh crumbs, does it show? I must watch it.' Wendy wrinkled her delicate nose. 'Sour grapes, perhaps.' She paused before re-locking the surgery door. 'You're not wanting to go in, Bob? Fine. So, where have you two sprung from?'

'Friars Court ... just a working dinner since Charlotte's going to be tied up on Friday,' Robert explained.

'Yes, nothing earth-shaking,' Charlotte repeated with a smile.

'Well, if you want to talk some more,' Wendy said, 'come back to my place for a nightcap and you can fill me in on the useful bits.'

Charlotte smothered a convenient yawn. 'At the risk of sounding unsociable, do you mind if I don't? It's been a long day. We only came back here to collect my car.' (In truth she was not at all tired, but two's company—three's a crowd, she thought. Robert could answer for himself.)

'Fair enough.' Wendy made no attempt to try to persuade her. 'How about you, Bob?'

'OK, you've talked me into it,' he replied amiably.

The three of them walked towards their cars and Robert paused alongside Charlotte's while she delved into her shoulder bag for her keys. 'Thank you for a lovely evening,' she said a little shyly, 'I really enjoyed it.'

'Me too.' He hesitated. 'You know, this is a bit awkward. By rights I should be following you home, to make sure you get there safely.'

'Don't be silly. I'll be fine. I've been driving myself around for yonks.'

'We-ell,' he growled, 'don't stop to pick up any vagrants on the way, will you?'

She grinned and on impulse reached to plant a featherlight kiss on his cheek. 'I promise, if only to clear your conscience.'

For answer he took her chin in a firm hand and kissed her squarely on the mouth. 'Pay your respects properly, or not at all. Lips are for kissing . . . cheeks are only for turning . . . sometimes,' he added. 'Something I'm not too good at, I must admit.'

Charlotte was still recovering from the electrifying effect of his mouth on hers. 'What—kissing or cheek turning?' she asked, making a joke of it.

'I was thinking about you having to give your support to this fellow on Friday, when you must feel like kicking him from here to kingdom come.'

She laughed. 'Oh, no, I don't. I totally agree with what you said about not bearing grudges—although I'll probably slam a few doors here and there to relieve my feelings.' It sounded convincing, even if it wasn't absolutely true.

Wendy pipped her horn just then, and Robert signalled to her that her was coming. 'Musn't keep the lady waiting,' he murmured. 'Sorry you decided not to join us, but it would have been rather out of your way, I suppose.' He shut Charlotte into her car and let her go.

On the short journey back to her own home the events of the evening were sufficient to push even the court case to the back of Charlotte's mind. It had somehow never occured to her that Robert might have been married, or that he had suffered a traumatic upheaval far more involved than her own. It explained a lot. No wonder he preferred to go it alone from now on. And now that she knew, it ought to make things easier between them. For instance she would know that if he sought her out it was simply because he liked her company and saw her as an acceptable working partner. Nothing more than that.

It was probably the same with Wendy, too; a friendly working relationship. Although whether Wendy viewed it like that was another matter. And thinking of Wendy, that was an odd reason for her to give—*sour grapes*—as her excuse for not being too keen on children. Why sour grapes? Was it just a pose—or was there an explanation for her attitude? Perhaps she couldn't have children? Perhaps it was a self-protective device because she saw them as a threat to her career? In any case, not every woman was enamoured with the idea of motherhood.

Arriving back at the house in Spinney Lane, Charlotte dismissed her own imaginings. She was most likely making a great mystery out of a casual throwaway remark. One thing was clear though, Wendy did have a soft spot for Robert. Fine, and it was no concern of Charlotte's. She would just get on with her own job, live her own life, and keep her own sexual impulses under stricter control. In retrospect, kissing the man—even playfully—was a stupid thing to do. Especially since it prompted him to return it with good measure. If Wendy had seen them, goodness knows what she would have made of it.

Charlotte sighed as she went up to bed. Too bad, she mused, that you just couldn't switch off when someone as fascinating as Robert hove into view and started making waves. She went to sleep brooding about him, wondering about his young daughter and how she felt about her absentee dad. She wondered whether Robert was really as reconciled to the way things were as he made out.

* * *

The following day Charlotte had no contact with Robert whose turn it was to function at the Valley Hospital. For her it was a kind of anticlimax, and time dragged although she had plenty to keep herself occupied. Oddly, merely the sight of his empty surgery made her feel dispirited.

Returning home that evening she found a small posy of anemones on the doorstep, and attached was a note in childish handwriting:

'Thank you for helping Mummy and me, Love Debby.'

Quite touched, after putting the flowers in water, she knocked next door to see if anyone was at home, and was welcomed by the child and her grandmother.

'Hallo, my love,' Mrs Dent said warmly. 'I've just brewed up. Will you come in?'

'Well, just for a moment,' Charlotte smiled, 'and you can tell me the latest news.' She had heard indirectly that Marjorie Clifton was responding to treatment, but nothing about the domestic arrangements, and Mrs Dent was obviously bursting to talk.

Around the kitchen table and the strongest cup of tea she'd ever had, Charlotte heard that Marjorie's husband had been to see her and that there had been a sort of truce. Mrs Dent was keeping her fingers crossed that something good would come out of it all.

'So you got to see you dad, did you?' Charlotte asked the bright-eyed Debby.

The little girl nodded. 'Yes, and he's coming again, next weekend if he can. But it's an awful long way, so he can't promise.'

'He says he's due some holiday when this job is

finished,' explained Mrs Dent. 'We'll have to take it from there.' She raised her eyes to heaven. 'I don't know!' Dropping the subject, she pointed to an empty ashtray on the dresser. 'What about that? I read those leaflets you gave me, and I tried cutting down on the ciggies, but that didn't work. So I've given up altogether.'

'Good for you!' Charlotte enthused. 'How long is it since you had a smoke?'

'A whole week! That's not long, I know,' the woman said, 'but I'm determined to stick it out. I mean, it's willpower really, isn't it? And I can hardly lay the law down to other folks about not trying hard enough if I can't fight my own battles, can I?' she added meaningfully.

Charlotte smiled. 'Well, that's one way of looking at it.' She went back home heartened that at least things seemed to be moving in the right direction there.

Her solitary meal that evening—broccoli au gratin from the freezer cabinet at the local store—was a very different affair from last night's first-class meal with Robert. She found herself wondering if he would be eating alone tonight, and where. It was common knowledge that he was living in hotel accommodation for the time being, and she supposed there would be restaurant facilities, or some good-hearted landlady to fuss over him. The Dales were full of hospitable guest houses and a good-looking, unattached professional man would be made more than welcome.

Feeling the need to talk, Charlotte decided now would be a convenient time to phone Lynne and, carrying her coffee through to the deep window-seat she dialled the number.

'Where've you been?' came her friend's voice over the wires. 'I tried ages last night to get you, but no luck. Did you have a date with Bryan?'

'No, that was Saturday. Last night it was a working dinner with Robert.'

'My goodness! You *are* popular,' laughed Lynne. 'Time I came back and kept an eye on you.' Without pausing for breath, she went on to explain that she had thought of coming back to Niddborough at the weekend. Nice though it was to be made a fuss of at home, she missed her own circle of friends.

'Ken, you mean,' Charlotte teased.

'Yeah, him too. He says I've only to let him know when and he'll collect me.' Lynne gave an ecstatic sigh. 'Lotty, we had a gorgeous weekend—I'm still pinching myself. Amazingly, even my dad approved and said Ken had more between his ears than some of the fellers I've taken home. I'm beginning to think it may be the real thing. Anyway, hopefully it won't be too long now before my plaster comes off, so I wouldn't be too much of a strain to have around, would I?'

'Of course not,' Charlotte reassured her. 'I'm missing you already. Come back . . . all is forgiven!' she joked. 'Actually there's been so much going on around here I've hardly had time to breathe since you left.'

She launched into a detailed account of all the happenings, and finally to her own forthcoming trip to London at the weekend. 'I have to go Thursday night, but I'll leave stuff in the fridge, Lynne, and if you're back before I am, I'm quite sure Mrs Dent would give you a hand if you needed it. She's staying next door to look after Debby until her mum comes out of hospital.'

'Wow!' exclaimed Lynne. 'That's never happened to me, thank goodness. Having to be a witness, I mean. How do you feel about it?'

'A bit jittery, in case I say the wrong thing. I wouldn't like it to be my fault if it went against Phil.'

'Do you think the claimants have a case?' Lynne asked.

'They shouldn't have a hope—but if they get a good barrister, who knows? I'll be glad when it's all over,' Charlotte declared with feeling.

'Where've you got to go?' Lynne queried.

'It's at the Law Courts in the Strand. I'll stay overnight with Amy at the old Bayswater flat, but I shan't hang around once it's all over. I've had my fill of London.'

'Mmm,' mused Lynne, 'I suppose it's been a bit difficult, having to talk to Phil about it.'

Charlotte let out a long resigned breath. 'I haven't, yet. I don't even know where he's working at the moment. It was the solicitor who got in touch with me.'

She herself had thought it a bit off, to say the least, that Phil hadn't bothered to get in touch himself. Nevertheless, she was quite startled when she picked up the phone shortly afterwards and heard his deeply resonant voice with its attractive Welsh overtones.

'Carlotta, my love, is that really you?'

He had always called her Carlotta, and bittersweet memories came to mind at the sound of it. 'Hallo,

Phil,' she returned levelly. 'And how are you?'

'Physically, fine. Mentally, up the creek with the court case hanging over me. We were hoping they would pull out before it went this far. But I hear you're going to give me your support, and I wanted to thank you personally, my love. You're a trump.'

'Oh, I wouldn't wish even my worst enemy to be unjustly condemned,' she returned drily.

'Is that how you think of me, as your worst enemy?' he asked, in a softly cajoling tone. 'I know I deserved it, but darling girl, I'm a reformed character now, so *please* don't.'

She could picture the coaxing expression on his dark, intelligent face and felt his words wrap around her like a soothing balm. Then Robert Challoner's dark good looks also rose to mind, the resolute jaw, and the forthright advice he had given her . . . Let him see he didn't even dent your ego! . . . and with a light laugh she returned, 'Of course I don't, Phil. There's no time to waste on regretting the past. I'm far too busy keeping up with the present.'

'I'm most relieved to hear it. You were my one wild oat, sweetheart, and very precious, believe me. Strange though it may seem, I'm a respectable pillar of society these days. Faithful unto death and all that. My son is four months old, and he's a real cracker.'

His self-satisfaction was obvious. She let him ramble on, only half hearing much of what he said as her thoughts went back to the old days.

She gathered that he had now got his fellowship and was a surgical registrar at St Benedict's with a home of his own in North London. Naturally, the last thing he wanted at this stage of the game was a lot of adverse publicity.

'Too bad the fellow refused to sign that self-discharge, but fortunately the facts were well recorded in Sister Pointer's night report at the time, and my own report was countersigned by the houseman,' Phil continued. 'All the evidence is in my favour, but you know how blind the public can be when they see the pound signs beckoning. So your own evidence will be invaluable.'

'Phil, I understand,' she said patiently. 'I'll do my best for you.'

'Good girl, and afterwards let's hope we can have a celebratory drink together, eh?'

'That depends. I won't be able to hang about. I'll need to get back as soon as possible,' Charlotte told him.

'Oh, *sorry*,' he sighed, 'I've been gassing away about my own affairs and never even asked how things are with you. Everything all right? What are doing these days? How's your love-life?'

'Everything's terrific, thanks, but I can't stop to talk now, Phil. A friend's just arrived.'

'Aha!' he said with heavy innuendo. 'Say no more! Tell him from me he's a lucky guy. See you Friday, pet.'

It was a relief to slam down the phone and let the tears come. As well as being disturbed she was fighting mad. Trust Phil to automatically assume her 'friend' was a man. Of course, no one had arrived and she wasn't expecting anyone, but it would certainly do him no harm to think so. Of course she liked masculine company as much as the next girl, but she wasn't pining away for lack of it!

Charlotte went back to the kitchen, grabbed a piece of kitchen roll and blew her nose vigorously. *Men*! she thought with contempt, they couldn't bear to think that a girl could get along without them. They thought you sized up every guy with a view to marriage. Drying her eyes, she decided on another cup of coffee to pull herself together. Maybe it wasn't a bad thing to have had a little weep now—get it out of her system. Then perhaps she would be less uptight when she actually had to meet Phil again.

Waiting for the kettle to boil, she sniffed and brushed away a last tear. She was glad she was alone—at least she could cheer up in her own good time. Presently she would get out her paints and do a bit more to that sketch of irises she was halfway through. All tender lilac, and mauve with touches of amethyst. She found painting deliciously therapeutic—guaranteed to take her mind off other things.

A peremptory ring at the doorbell made her start. Who the dickens could that be at nine o'clock? A collector for charity possibly, or a pools rep, or a double-glazing salesman. If she ignored it they'd go away. She finished making her coffee.

The caller rang again. Carrying her drink into the living-room, Charlotte peeped through the window, and her stomach lurched. Robert Challoner's car was drawn up outside. And with her own car parked there, and lights on in the house, he would guess she was home, so she could hardly leave him to take it out on the doorbell. Disinclined to talk to anyone, least of all *him* in her present mood, Charlotte composed her features and went to face him.

'Hello!' she exclaimed, professing surprise. 'Not

again! I should have thought you'd had enough of me last night.'

He was eyeing her quizzically with that air of quiet authority which undermined all her feminist resolutions. Her colour heightened as she saw him taking in the evidence of her recent tears. Obviously her eye make-up must be a total mess. She laughed self-consciously. 'I've just been watching a weepy on the box. Bet I look like a panda, don't I?'

'Or a Black-eyed Susan,' he returned with a flicker of humour about the corners of his mouth. Reaching into his jacket pocket, he produced a small brown plastic wallet which she recognised immediately as containing her driving licence and credit cards. 'Your property, I believe?'

'Good heavens!' Her mouth sagged a little as she opened it to check the contents. 'I hadn't even missed it. Where did you find it?'

'On the floor of my car—you must have dropped it last night. I didn't discover it until this evening or I would have been in touch before.'

'Well, thanks,' she said. 'Good of you to come. A-are you on your rounds . . . or what?'

'Just or what. And yes, I would like a coffee if you thought of offering me one.'

'Of course. Come in.' She switched on a smile, being polite and welcoming when she would really have liked to be slamming doors. For goodness' sake, why couldn't she be alone and extravagantly miserable if she wanted to be?

CHAPTER SEVEN

HAVE YOU eaten, or would you like a sandwich?' Charlotte enquired, her natural good manners prevailing.

'No, nothing to eat, thanks, just a coffee. And do you mind if I make a quick phone call to Mac while you're getting it?' Robert asked.

'Not at all.' She waved him towards the living-room. 'Help yourself.'

She took her time making the coffee, seizing the opportunity to tidy up her face a bit, muttering a few invectives under her breath in the process. She felt embarrassed and irritated. He *would* have to come busting in on her unannounced, wouldn't he! Of course, she knew she was being unreasonable. If she hadn't dropped her belongings Robert wouldn't have come, so she had only herself to blame for this intrusion into her privacy.

All the same, Charlotte ruminated, she was entitled to a life of her own, wasn't she? Not in this close-knit community, apparently! It was getting to be almost as bad as hospital life where the slightest rumour spread like wildfire, and gathered a few frills on the way. Well, she couldn't be bothered with entertaining tonight. He could just take her as he found her.

Robert had finished his telephone call by the time she took his drink through. 'Sorry I interrupted your television programme,' he said, lowering his long frame into one of the deep armchairs. 'If it was a tear-jerker, perhaps I did you a favour, though,' he added with a disarming grin. 'What were you watching?'

She would not allow herself to be charmed. Nor need he think he was going to sit there for the rest of the evening, seducing her senses. 'Actually, that wasn't true. I wasn't watching anything,' she admitted, not caring a toss what he thought. 'I was feeling a bit fragile over something. Being self-indulgent.'

'Oh! I see.' He stirred his drink, offering no sympathy, just watching her with those discerning blue eyes of his which seemed to pierce beyond the physical and into every corner of her mind. 'Well,' he said after a moment, 'it takes more muscle power to frown than it does to smile, so why not cheer up and save yourself some energy?'

She had seated herself on a cushion on the floor to drink her own coffee, now half-cold, and that didn't please her either. 'I don't particularly want to,' she said. 'There's nothing in the rules that says I have to be laughing for twenty-four hours a day, is there?'

He made a comic face, pulled a white handkerchief from his jacket pocket and waved it at her. 'Unconditional surrender suit you?'

She tried hard not to smile and didn't quite succeed.

'Might one ask if there's any particular reason for this wave of self-indulgence?' Robert hazarded.

'Yes. I came to the conclusion that he's a bastard.'

'Er . . . now which particular *he* is that . . . Jack-the-lad?'

'Who else?'

'Well, we knew that months ago, didn't we? So what's new?'

'As you say—nothing,' Charlotte agreed. 'It's just me being slow to catch on.'

'Oh, I wouldn't call you slow on the uptake.' Robert studied her with a mixture of curiosity and clinical detachment. At least, Charlotte imagined that was what it was. 'We've all been very impressed with your powers of observation,' he told her. 'but what brought about this sudden revelation? Has something happened?'

She told him about her call from Phil in connection with the court case. 'He's so disgustingly smug, him and his Happy Families,' she complained, gritting her pearly teeth. 'Men never lose out, do they? Oh, sorry, I was forgetting *you* did, didn't you?'

He scratched his cheek, considering. 'At the time, yes. But in the long term I would say I've gained. The new career it started me on is something I've never regretted. That's a plus for me—whether it is for the population at large is another matter,' he added with a half-smile. 'Now, what can we do to raise your morale? You wouldn't fancy looking in on Mac and Naomi? He says they could do with a little light relief from the cares of parenthood. I gather Naomi's disenchanted with being a twenty-four-hour milk machine.'

Charlotte was almost tempted. 'I haven't seen their baby yet and I'd love to—but not tonight, Robert. I couldn't make the effort to be suitably worshipping.'

'OK. What else can I suggest? Scrabble—draughts—tiddlywinks?'

She laughed. 'Look, you don't have to worry about me. I'm fine—really. Just push off and amuse yourself.'

'But I *am* amusing myself,' he returned. 'I find your company quite diverting. You're constantly presenting me with challenges.'

'Glad to be of service. I'll see what else I can dream up,' she said in the same facetious manner.

'Seriously,' Robert continued, 'is there anything you *would* like to do?'

Charlotte hugged her knees, her expression pensive. 'What I'd really like to do you'll probably think completely screwy. Go for a walk in the woods and listen to the silence. Times like this I wish I had a dog.'

'As a matter of fact, that's not a bad idea. At least it's not quite as drastic as my Ben Nevis solution.' Easing himself out of the chair, the doctor stretched expansively, widening his broad chest. 'If I'll do instead of the dog, come on, let's go.'

He reached down from his six-foot-three to help her to her feet. With her hands held fast in his, Charlotte felt his power irradiating her senses. Warm and secure? Or exciting and dangerous? Why did she land herself in these difficult situations?

'No, forget it,' she said with an uncertain laugh. 'I was only being fanciful.'

Turning her by the shoulders, he prodded her towards the door. 'Go on . . . get some shoes on . . . and you'll need a sweater, won't you?'

'We-ell, if you're sure . .' It seemed churlish to argue and so, despite her qualms, Charlotte ran upstairs to get ready. She really did fancy getting out of the house. A walk in the cool night air would clear her mind of the unwelcome clutter which her talk with Phil had aroused. Unfortunately a girl could hardly go walking in the woods by herself late at night. It was decent of Robert to humour her when he must have had a busy day.

She had been padding around in stripey socks and a pink cotton playsuit. Now she hurriedly searched out a pair of trainers from the bottom of the wardrobe and knotted the sleeves of a bright blue sweater around her shoulders. Keep calm—no need to flap, she told herself, grimacing at her flushed image in the mirror. She pulled a comb through her tousled fair hair, fluffing it around her face. There was nothing significant in Robert's gesture; he was merely being accommodating. And so long as he wasn't aware of the furore he set up inside her, no harm done.

'All fit then?' he asked amiably when she rejoined him. 'Right. Where are you taking me? Should I be in training for this? I didn't know you were a hiker.'

Pulling the front door to behind them, Charlotte laughed and strove to control the waves of tension in her tummy. 'I'm not. In fact I turned down an invitation from Bryan to join his rambling club the other day. Gentle strolls are more my style.'

Her reason for mentioning Bryan was to remind Robert that she was a free spirit from choice, like himself, just in case he'd forgotten. She didn't want him to misconstrue her motives. Quite truthfully, she had spoken off the top of her head without thinking and with no idea that he'd actually take her up on this crazy impulse.

At the mention of Bryan's name, however, Robert

merely gave a noncommittal grunt before saying, 'Where do we start ... do you want to drive somewhere first?'

'Oh, no!' Charlotte laughed, 'the little woods at the top of the lane will be fine.'

'OK, whatever you say. A nice gentle stroll it is, then.'

They fell into step side by side at a leisurely pace, walking in the road since that was easier than along the narrow grassy pavement. Spinney Lane wound itself upwards away from the town, lit by infrequent street lamps along its half-mile length. At ten-thirty the night was dark but not black. The sky reflected the glow from a myriad lights of habitation, and the moon sailed in and out of fleecy grey clouds, shedding a silvery radiance over the quiet landscape.

After the last lamp-post and the last lonely house, the lane petered out into a well-trodden footpath on the fringes of Three-corner Wood, an oasis of stately beech and birch trees where bluebells grew in undisturbed profusion. The flowers were dying now, standing like little ghosts of the spring, but their sweetness still lingered on the soft night air.

Somewhere along the way Robert had taken Charlotte's hand when she stumbled over a rut, but they walked in silence, both engrossed in their own thoughts. Twigs crackled beneath their feet and centuries of fallen beech-mast added an earthy perfume to the atmosphere. The wood was full of the steathly sounds of night creatures—a rustling, a sleepy stirring, a distant muted cry. It was a magic place where anything might happen, Charlotte felt. And with her was a man whose very handhold sent fire through her veins. She wondered how he could not be aware of it.

With a sudden clatter of wings and a long churring cry, a large brown shape rose from the undergrowth and dived across their path.

They both stopped short for a moment. 'What bird was that?' Robert asked.

It served to relax her tension although her limbs had been trembly even before the surprise intruder. She drew a deep, steadying breath. 'Probably a nightjar after moths. You rarely see them . . .'

He squeezed her hand and smiled at her. 'Did it startle you?'

'Just a bit,' she laughed, 'But I'm a country girl, I should be used to country sounds.' She smiled back at him, feeling it best to keep the conversation going. 'How about you?'

'Me? Oh, I'm just a towny who likes the best of both worlds. The pleasures of the countryside and the convenience of the city. Is it possible to have both?'

'More and more possible these days, with motorways cutting down the miles. That's if one doesn't destroy the other.'

His arm slid round her waist as they walked on, talking with ease now.

'Where were you born?' she wanted to know.

'Hampstead. The Heath was my playground. A great place to be near for London kids, but hardly equivalent to the grandeur of the Dales.'

His parents, he told her, still lived in Hampstead. His father worked in the City and his mother taught at a primary school. 'I'm their one and only . . . and they regret their lost granddaughter.'

'Mmm, I'm sure they do,' she returned. 'Do you go home much?'

'Not as often as I should. But the telephone helps, doesn't it? I keep in touch.'

They had come to the end of the enchanted wood and as if for a finale, a rich, fluting bird-song burst upon the air, its striking repertoire of liquid cadences alternating with the softest, most endearing of throaty warblings.

'That's a nightingale!' Charlotte breathed. 'Isn't it exquisite?'

Almost as exquisite as the girl beside him, the doctor thought. And this place—it was as haunting and magical as the legendary island of *Bali Ha'i.* He had to remind himself that he was a good ten years older than his companion, and that she was in a susceptible state of mind at the moment; too vulnerable to be toyed with.

Resisting his overwhelming desire to kiss her small upturned face, like a pale flower in the darkness, Robert pulled her supple body a little closer and followed her gaze in the direction of the outpouring. 'A bit off course for Berkeley Square, isn't he?' he quipped.

'Oh, you! Where's your soul?' She wrinkled her nose at him. 'Philistine!'

'Well, one of us has to keep our feet on the ground,' he teased. 'My part in this excursion is purely protect-tive. Time I got you back to base, don't you think?'

'Yes, I suppose so.' With an effort Charlotte dragged herself back to reality while the unseen small brown bird let forth another burst of brilliance to bewitch her. They had emerged opposite rolling grasslands with the characteristic drystone walls criss-crossing the fields. 'If we follow this road round it'll lead us back to Spinney Lane. It won't take long if we step it out—there's a right of way alongside the cricket ground,' she went on.

Purely for the purpose of preventing stumbles over the dark country road, Robert continued to hold her hand on their purposeful walk back. He also lifted her down from the stile they had to cross on re-entering Spinney Lane. The act set her nerves alight as their bodies brushed. For one brief moment their faces were so close it would have taken no effort for their lips to come together, but Robert released her abruptly.

'Being practical,' he said when they walked on, 'How are you proposing to go to London on Thursday—will you drive?'

'No, I shall go on the Inter-City from York.'

'And how will you get to York?'

'Oh, train. Or bus. I haven't checked the times yet, but I'd like to catch the five-fifteen from York, if that's convenient.'

'We'll make it convenient. You'd best take the afternoon off, and if you need any help, you must let me know.'

'Thank you, but I expect I shall manage.'

'Oh, I'm sure you will.' He darted her a sharp look from under his frowning brows. ' . . . But if you can't, don't be too obstinate to ask. You can take this independence lark too far, you know.'

Charlotte shrugged. 'No offence, and it isn't a lark. I really am quite capable of finding my own way around. That's not to say I haven't appreciated your company tonight,' she put in quickly. 'It was lovely, wasn't it? The walk, I mean. Thanks for coming.'

They were back at the house now and he paused beside his car, studying her critically with his dark head on one side. 'Did it have the desired effect? Are you soothed and restored?'

'Yes. I shall sail through the rest of the week.'

His rather stern expression lightened. He was still tempted to wrap her in his arms and kiss the breath out of her. 'Well, it was a somewhat novel expererience for me,' he said, keeping his hands firmly under control, 'We must do it again some time. But don't be silly enough to try it on your own late at night, will you? Going to let yourself in before I push off?' He found his key to unlock the car and stood waiting.

'Yes, I will. Goodbye, and thanks again.' She ran up the path, and let herself into the house, switched on the lights and turned to wave to him.

He returned her salute and she heard him start his engine as she closed the front door.

As she took herself upstairs to bed Charlotte's thoughts were in chaos. She certainly wasn't soothed, although she was, in a way, oddly elated. And she wasn't restored, in fact she felt quite drained. True, out there in the dark woods there had been mystical, uplifting moments. But the delight had been fraught with disaster, for if Robert had felt inclined to make love to her she couldn't have resisted. Her body ached for him. She longed to have his alluring mouth search for hers. And surely he must have known it, because there was quite definitely a certain empathy between them. He either had the most amazing self-control or she just didn't turn him on in that way.

Whichever it was she felt cheated. It must be purely

physical attraction on her part. Robert's fantastic body and fascinating personality—that heady mixture of arrogance and chivalry—was guaranteed to knock any girl off her feet. Oh well, since nothing happened, thank goodness, there would be nothing to regret. The trouble was even if you had decided against another emotional involvement, you couldn't turn off your wretched sex hormones. Those things that could change sensible people into emotional halfwits.

She couldn't actually be falling for the man, could she? Chartlotte didn't really need to answer that, and the truth brought her dismay. She slung her trainers back into the bottom of the wardrobe. Blow sex-hormones! Blow the whole rotten male/female business! she thought stormily. You just couldn't win.

On Wednesday evening, having checked the times of her trains, Charlotte decided what to wear for her London trip and packed her overnight bag in readiness. Once her work at the Health Centre was finished the following morning all she would have to do was to shoot home, have a spot of lunch, get ready and go.

All went smoothly at work the next day. In between patients she was able to get ahead with labelling and packaging her specimens for the laboratory, and leaving everything in order for the part-time nurse who would be standing in for her.

There was still a small private matter Charlotte had on her mind, and with a few minutes to spare she took out and re-read the letter which had come for her by the morning post. It was from Aunt Hannah, straight to the point in her aunt's usual blunt fashion:

I have a small health problem which I don't care to discuss with our own GP since he is a personal friend of the Major's and I should find it embarrassing. I believe there is a woman doctor in your set-up. Do you think you could pull a few strings and arrange for her to see me privately, fairly soon? Say one afternoon next week? And don't say anything to anyone else about this. I'll wait to hear from you.

Best love, Hannah.

Wondering what the problem could be and hoping she would have the chance to speak to Wendy that morning, Charlotte was quite pleased when the doctor rang to ask for her assistance.

In the surgery with Wendy was a middle-aged woman. She had a badly-bruised eye socket and extensive dirty and bleeding abrasions down one side of her face.

'Dear me!' exclaimed Charlotte in sympathy. 'That looks nasty.'

'Yes—Mrs Cooper fell off her bicycle in an unmade road,' Wendy explained with due concern. 'I'd like you to clean it up as much as you can, please, and put a dressing on. And she's never been immunised for tetanus, so she must have a course of active vaccine.' Wendy wrote her instructions on the case notes. 'The first dose stat, IM, and the usual follow-up. We can't be too careful in the country. You go with Nurse, Mrs Cooper, she'll look after you. And come back and see us in a week.'

Taking the patient back to her treatment room, Charlotte started the laborious and painful business of thoroughly cleansing the grazes with a Savlon solution. Even with her expert and gentle hands it was impossible not to hurt sometimes. 'Sorry about that, love,' she apologised as the woman bit her lip, trying to be brave, 'but I have to get as much of this grime out as possible.'

Having done the best she could, she applied a sterile, non-adhesive dressing to the raw area and gave the required intramuscular injection.

'As Dr Fenner explained, it's important to be immunised against tetanus with all the farm traffic about in this area. You'll need another two injections, the next one in about six weeks. I'll send you a reminder.' Charlotte leafed through her diary and made a note against a suitable date. It was fairly obvious that the woman had been considerably shaken by her accident, and Charlotte asked kindly, 'How are you going to get home, Mrs Cooper? Is anyone with you?'

'Yes, thank you, Nurse. My son brought me in his car,' the patient replied in a lack-lustre voice. 'He's waiting outside.'

'Oh, that's good. You have a nice cup of tea and take it easy when you get back. Try not to disturb the dressing, but if it should come loose, just drop in and I'll fix it again for you.'

After seeing the unfortunate housewife on her way, Charlotte cleaned up her dressings trolley and washed her hands. The waiting area was now empty of patients and the receptionist had gone to lunch.

Hoping to grab Wendy before she, too, disappeared, Charlotte knocked and popped her head around the surgery door. She found the doctor sitting at her desk with her chin on her hands, her normally serene face a study in despondency.

'Come in, Charlotte,' she said wearily. 'You managed that job all right, did you?'

'Yes, poor Mrs Cooper. I'm afraid it was a bit excruciating for her. Er . . . sorry to disturb you, Wendy. Are you all right?'

'Yes, personally I'm fine. God's in his heaven, but all's *not* right with the world, I'm sorry to say.'

'Anything I can do?'

The doctor looked at the patient's notes in front of her. 'Nothing that you, or I, or anyone can do. The amniocentesis test shows that this lass is expecting a male child.' She tapped the folder. 'There's a familial history of haemophilia, and she's a carrier. You know what that means—a fifty-fifty chance of the boy being born a bleeder.' Wendy ran a despairing hand through her thick dark hair. 'I offered her a termination and she's gone away to think about it.'

'Oh dear,' murmured Charlotte, 'and I suppose she's desperate for a baby.'

'Yes. I've laid it on the line what she'll be letting herself in for if she goes ahead. I should know . . . it's in my own family.'

Charlotte frowned. 'In your family?'

Wendy put the notes in her out-tray and nodded. 'My own brother died two years ago. The result of a road accident, from which he bled to death despite massive transfusions. I'm a carrier,' she went on, 'and knowing the problems he faced all through his life I long ago decided never to perpetuate the disease myself. No kids for me.'

Charlotte was shocked. So *that* was what Wendy had meant by 'sour grapes' when speaking of children. Should she ever become pregnant there would be a fifty per cent risk her sons would be 'bleeders' and an equal risk that her daughters, like herself, would pass on the disease to their own offspring. Poor Wendy. When faced with that kind of tragedy, Charlotte felt her own little problems seemed minimal. And to say she was sorry seemed so trite.

For a moment she was speechless. She shook her head and said, 'That's rotten.' Trying to be encouraging, she went on, 'but I suppose the prognosis is a little better now than when your brother was born.'

'Oh yes, research is making headway, but you know how long these things take. Well?' Wendy flashed a smile, 'what did you want with me?'

Charlotte's own mission had slipped to the back of her mind, grappling with the doctor's traumatic disclosure. 'Oh, it's about my Aunt Hannah . . .' She fished the letter out of her pocket. 'I've no idea what the problem is. All I can tell you is that she's forty-eight and that she got married for the first time about five months ago. Could you fit her in one day next week?'

'Sit down a minute while I check.' Wendy looked through her diary. 'Thursday - two-thirty?'

'Great. I'll tell her, thanks.'

'My pleasure. Perhaps she just wants a woman-to-woman talk,' the doctor said with a whimsical smile, 'and I don't blame her. Sometimes I think there must be more male chauvinists in the medical profession than anywhere else. Barring Mac and Bob, of course, although even they can be obtuse when it suits them.' Her eyes sparkled with mischief. 'I hear you took Bob birdwatching last night.'

Charlotte's mouth dropped open, then she laughed. 'Yes, that's how it turned out. Don't ask me how or why. It just happened.'

'That's the way it goes sometimes,' Wendy said lightly. 'Oh well, my half-day.' She locked her desk. 'I'm going to Harrogate to buy some clothes. You wouldn't like to come?'

'Love to, but I can't. I'm off to London on the five-fifteen from York,' 'Charlotte reminded her.

'Ah yes, your friend's litigation case. Well, good luck, and say hallo to Harrods for me if you get the time. London!' Wendy blew a kiss from her fingertips. 'I adore it.'

'You can have my share,' Charlotte returned.

She left the doctor's office feeling that she knew Wendy a little better and liking her a lot. With some people, she mused, it was instant rapport, while with others it took time to break the ice. First impressions could be misleading. And whatever Wendy's relationship with Robert, she hadn't seemed to mind about the so-called birdwatching.

Hanging her keys behind the reception desk, Charlotte set off for home in a cheerful frame of mind. Once indoors, before doing anything else, she rang Hannah to say she had made the appointment.

'Thank you, Charlotte. That didn't take you

long,' her aunt approved. 'I shall have to tell Oliver I'm having a day's shopping and coming on to see you afterwards.'

'There's nothing seriously wrong, I hope?' Charlotte asked.

'No, no! Well, at least, I'm not sure . . .' The older woman paused. 'I feel well enough. Never felt better, but . . . Oh, wait until I've seen the doctor. No point in speculating. And for goodness' sake, don't say a word to anyone about this, will you?'

Charlotte promised her discretion and asked no more questions, concluding it must be some feminine problem which her aunt was reluctant to discuss with a man. Time would tell. Meantime she had best get a move on or she would miss that train.

CHAPTER EIGHT

NOT KNOWING exactly how long she would be away, Charlotte had chosen to leave her car at home and take a taxi to the local station for her connection to York. Allowing a little extra time, she got the driver to drop her off at the chemist's shop in the High Street, so that she could buy a thank-you gift for Amy.

In the dispensary area—a raised platform at the far end of the shop—the white-coated Bryan was busy making up prescriptions. He glanced across and saw Charlotte, who gave him a friendly wave.

Having bought some luxury bath oil, she bent down to tuck it into her overnight bag, and Bryan, after placing a completed order on a shelf, came down to the front of the counter to join her.

'Been meaning to ring you.' he breezed. 'What are you doing on Saturday night?'

'Actually, I'm just on my way to London for the weekend ... looking up some of my old mates,' she told him, not bothering with details.

'Oh, pity' he grinned again and his enquiring eyes lingered over her stylish cinnamon suit and cream silk blouse. 'Thought you looked all dressed up. I was going to ask you if you fancied coming to a concert—it's a Barbershop Quartet Festival.'

'Mmm—that's different,' she said with a smile. 'Sorry I can't make it. Are you doing your usual organising thing?'

'Yes—the usual crowd. I can see I shall have to give you more notice if we're to have the pleasure of your company.'

They stayed talking for a few more minutes until Charlotte looked at the clock. 'Is that the right time? I shall have to dash, Bryan, or I shall miss my train.'

'Righto. I'll give you an early ring next time there's anything special on,' he promised.

Every town should have a Bryan, she thought, smiling to herself as she nipped along the High Street. He was everybody's friend, always the same, nice and uncomplicated.

Almost at the station approach, she suddenly noticed the maroon BMW which pulled to a halt a few yards ahead of her. The next moment the driver alighted and the tall, powerful figure of Robert Challoner came striding towards her.

'Wasn't that well-timed?' he said, reaching a hand out for her bag. 'I take it you're on your way to York?'

'Yes I am, and my train's in five minutes.' Her stomach was doing ridiculous somersaults, making her feel breathless. She knew she was blushing, which made matters worse. 'Terribly sorry, I can't really stop.'

'What you can do is stop rattling on about trains!' he said, guiding her towards his car. 'I'm going to York myself. We can be there in under half an hour. You won't do it quicker than that on the train. Come on, I'm parked on a double yellow.'

'Robert, this is awfully kind of you, but you don't have to go out of your way for me . . .'

He raised impatient blue eyes to heaven. 'I'm

not going out of my way. I have to see someone at the hospital there. I didn't set out to meet you—it just happened. Come on, I obliged you with my company the other night. Aren't you going to return the favour?'

She smiled. 'We-ell, if you put it like that . . .'

'Hop in quickly, then.' He threw the bag into the back of the car and hissed, 'There's a traffic warden looming.'

She slid in and fastened her seat-belt. Meanwhile the doctor strolled around to the driver's seat, flung a heart-warming smile at the tubby warden on the other side of the road, and pulled away. 'It's all right,' he explained, 'I diagnosed her husband's diabetes. She thinks I'm wonderful. A good job someone does.'

Charlotte curbed a smile. 'Stop fishing for compliments.'

He negotiated the car past the busy market place and out on to the York road before he answered. 'Well, you won't need to fish for compliments in court tomorrow. And you wouldn't be the first pretty face to change the course of history. The opposition doesn't know what it's up against.'

She giggled. 'Oh, shut up. I don't want to talk about it. Bad enough when the time comes.'

'Anyone would think it was you going to be on trial instead of Jack-the-lad.'

'I wonder how he's feeling?' Charlotte pondered. 'Bound to be apprehensive. I suppose. although he didn't sound too worried.'

'Humph!' Robert grunted. 'Seems to me to be the kind of guy who could fall in a bog and come out whiter than white. But OK, let's forget it.'

'Yes. I had a rather surprising talk with Wendy today,' Charlotte went on chattily. 'She told me about her brother, the one who died after a road accident. I assume it was the brother you had dealings with when you first met her. The complicating factor you mentioned was his haemophilia, was it?'

Robert nodded. 'So she told you, did she? I don't think it's common knowledge. She carries her problems very close to her chest, which isn't really good for her. I'm glad she opened up. How did it arise?'

'She was telling me about a young pregnant patient of hers with a haemophiliac family history. Wendy said she would never risk having children herself because she's a carrier. Sad, isn't it? And with all the babies and youngsters she comes across in general practice, it must be like rubbing salt in the wound.'

'I know,' Robert agreed. 'A large slice of our work is concerned with giving birth or not giving birth, and so on.'

'And human nature being what it is, once there's a risk attached to it, that must make it seem as tempting as forbidden fruit. Poor Wendy,' Charlotte sighed.

'Mmm . . . It's a bigger problem than most of us ever have to contend with. She's fairly resigned to it, though, but that's what you'd expect from someone as self-controlled as Wendy.'

Charlotte watched the moving patterns of sunlight on the distant hills. 'As distinct from someone self-indulgent like me,' she murmured.

Slowing the car to filter into a roundabout, Robert gave her a sideways look. 'I didn't say that. It takes all sorts to make a world. We need the nutters who occasionally feel impelled to take off into the wild woods.'

She laughed softly. '... or want to go birdwatching, as you appear to have described it to Wendy.'

'Yes, I enjoyed my birdwatching session. Very educational. Apparently Wendy was trying to get hold of me that evening, which was how I came to tell her.' Robert hesitated. 'You two seem to have had a good old gossip. I shall have to watch my step.'

'Oh, that was just a passing comment while we were talking shop,' Charlotte put in. 'We were fixing up a private appointment for my Aunt Hannah. For some reason or other she wants to see a woman doctor instead of her own GP.'

'Why ... is your aunt ill? Or pregnant?'

Charlotte gulped, her green eyes widening. '*Pregnant*? Good heavens! That never even occurred to me. She's forty-eight.'

The doctor shrugged. 'So what?'

'So what?' echoed Charlotte as the possibility sank in. 'It's certainly an interesting idea.' She chewed her thumbnail thoughtfully.

'How welcome would that be?' Robert asked.

'I wouldn't know. There were too many years between us for that level of conversation. All I ever got from Hannah—when I was home from school for the holidays—were veiled warnings about what happened to Millie Coates in her father's barn and to make sure the same thing didn't happen to me. As nobody ever invited me into Farmer Coates' barn,

I'm still trying to figure out what I missed!' Charlotte joked.

Robert tutted and shook his head. 'They're a great responsibility, adolescent girls, and they're even more precocious across the Atlantic than they are here, which I worry about at times. A pointless excercise you might say, since my young daughter's sex education is out of my hands.'

'In any case, it's not really the kind of thing fathers and daughters talk about,' Charlotte pointed out.

They were nearing the outer limits of York now, leaving behind the open spaces for solid grey stone Victorian houses and warm brick villas in garden settings, many of them advertising Bed & Breakfast, or more grandly styled as private hotels.

'Whereabouts is your father's farm?' Robert wanted to know.

'Not this way—it's nearer to Ripon.'

'Oh! I was looking at some property near Boroughbridge.'

'Yes, it's nice there. Far enough, but not too far from the practice. Did you have any luck?'

'One or two possibilities.' The doctor dropped his speed as houses, shops and traffic became more congested. 'I'm biding my time for the moment. I may want your advice later. How long, may I ask, do you propose to desert us?'

'Only as long as it takes. Lynne is coming back some time this weekend, so I'll be home by Saturday if I can, in case she needs me.'

'What about if *we* need you?' Robert challenged. 'Your deputy is fine, very willing. But she's not Charlotte.'

She laughed. 'Oh, come off it. I bet half the time you don't even know I'm there.'

'Is that what you think? Well, young Charlotte, just you lay your ghost and come back to us as quick as you can. And be strong. Don't listen to any sob stories from Jack-the-lad about how much you always meant to him and how much he's missed you. *I* know the type.'

They approached the old walls of the medieval city and he swung the car sharply left past Mickelgate Bar, following the outer road round to the station.

'Will you kindly stop calling me *young* Charlotte?' she protested. 'I'm not looking for a father figure.'

He pulled to a halt in the car-park, switched off the engine and turned to look at her. 'Of course you're not. You've got a father, haven't you?' There was something in his voice that was almost like a caress. And those enthralling blue eyes looking into hers made her forget everything except how much she wanted to be where he was, all of the time.

'I'm sorry I can't stop to see you on to your train,' he went on, suddenly practical. 'Hurry back to us, won't you?'

And because her heart was pounding so fiercely, she took refuge in irony. 'Oh, isn't it nice to be loved and wanted!'

Climbing out, he took her bag from the back of the car and walked round to give it to her. 'You may mock, Miss Blythe,' he said, wagging a finger. 'Well, off you go, then ... and don't take *him* for any moonlight walks, will you?'

'I honestly don't make a habit of it.'

'Good.' He lifted her chin and kissed her. Only

briefly, but certainly not paternally . . .

For a moment she gazed back at him with her soul in her eyes. Then quickly she turned and walked away towards the station.

London's King's Cross Station that early June evening presented the usual mixed bag of humanity arriving, departing, or milling around the information boards. By eight o'clock Charlotte was one of the crowd surging off the long-distance train which had started its journey at Edinburgh.

After the two and a half hours it had taken to come from York, she was glad at last to be there. She had read a bit, tackled a crossword puzzle, had some coffee from the buffet. Mostly though, she had gazed out of the window daydreaming about a certain authoritative, blue-eyed doctor who had told her to hurry back, stupid though it was to attach any importance to that remark. He liked her because she was useful to him. She helped make his work run smoothly. His work was his life, and on his own admission there was no room for women other than as colleagues or patients.

Deliberately steering her thoughts away from Robert, she came back to the purpose of her visit, wondering how things would turn out for Phil. Her own qualms were coupled with her reluctance to meet him again, whereas she doubted that would bother him. His chief anxiety was bound to be the effect on his career. She wondered also whether his wife would be in court. That would be an added embarrassment. She would be heartily glad when the whole thing was over and she could get back to her own affairs . . .

Leaving the main line station, Charlotte descended to the Underground and made for the right route to Queensway. The silver tube train thundered into view and within half an hour she was emerging into the daylight of the busy Bayswater Road. The mixture of smart shops and restaurants, imposing mansions and the beckoning green vistas of Kensington Gardens was familiar territory. It seemed only yesterday that she had been part of it. There was the boutique where she had bought her black taffeta dress for the last nurses' ball, and there the little French bistro where Phil had taken her for a birthday dinner . . .

Threading her way through loitering sightseers, Charlotte turned off the main road and found the quiet square where many once opulent Regency houses were now occupied as flats. She came to the place where she had shared with Amy for a time, and skipped up the small flight of steps. Two chipped stone lions guarded the heavy front door. Patting one affectionately on the head, she rang the bell opposite her friend's nameplate.

Amy's rather plummy voice came over the intercom. 'Hallo?'

'Amy? It's me,' she called cheerfully.

'Oh, super! Come on up . . . door's open.'

Charlotte turned the handle and went inside, stepping past two students' bicycles propped up in the lobby, and climbing the worn red-carpeted staircase to the first floor. As she reached the landing the door of the flat opened.

'Hi!' she began, expecting to see Amy's cropped blonde-streaked head. The rest of her greeting died on her lips, because the person who welcomed her, arms outstretched, was not Amy. It was Phil!

Phil in the flesh, even more devastatingly handsome than the memory she'd carried around. Tall, broad-shouldered, slim-hipped, and with that hint of devilment in his dark eyes that could win over the starchiest of nursing officers, let alone impressionable young nurses.

'Surprise, surprise!' he exclaimed, a sensual grin on his smooth, chiselled features. 'Hallo, Carlotta!'

'Wh-what are you doing here?' Charlotte got out when she finally remembered how to open and close her mouth.

Amy, hovering just behind him, gave an eloquent shrug. 'He just descended on me, Lots. Hope you don't mind?'

'No, I'm just amazed the happy family man was let out on his own, that's all.'

Phil chuckled softly, taking the dig in good part. 'Now, now, little one. Sarcasm doesn't become you.' Putting an arm around her shoulders, he bounced a kiss off her cheek and they all went into the living-room.

'There was I, hoping for a good evening with my old buddy . . . and I find *you* here!' Charlotte complained. 'Amy, I'm dying for a coffee.'

'Oh, gosh, yes. You must be knackered. I'll get it while he does his explaining. That's your room if you want to dump your things,' Amy said, pointing the way, 'my flatmate's on holiday.'

Looking well pleased with life, Phil lowered himself comfortably into a chair while Charlotte went to take off her jacket and find some degree of composure. Well, she had to meet him some time, so it might as well be now as later. Having Amy there would help.

Going back to join him, she was quite amazed at his calm and carefree demeanour. 'What's all this about explaining?' she asked.

With a fond smile, he studied her engaging heart-shaped face, petulant now at finding him there. 'So . . .' he said, 'you came all this way to give me your support. Bless you! It's incredibly noble of you, angel.'

Impatiently Charlotte combed her fingers through her hair. 'I thought I hadn't any option. And for a man who's about to be sued for medical negligence, you look remarkably happy. Do you know something I don't?'

'Yes, my love. I won't keep you in suspense any longer. There ain't gonna be no court case. The charge had been dropped.'

Charlotte's mouth gaped open yet again. 'How's that?'

'The prosecuting QC wouldn't go ahead. Said the case was bound to be thrown out as having no substance. Apparently their witnesses had disappeared into the woodwork. The complainant was advised to withdraw, and she finally did. Terrific, isn't it?' Phil was over the moon.

'Well, thank goodness for that.' Charlotte heaved a huge sigh of relief. 'I felt all along it wasn't on, but . . .' She paused, her wide green eyes equivocal. 'So actually, I needn't have come after all? When did you know this?'

'I wasn't told until four-thirty this afternoon,' Phil assured her. 'My solicitor did try to phone you, but you must have been already on your way. Sorry about that, sweetheart.'

'Crumbs! What an awful waste of time and money—the fare was enormous,' Charlotte lamented. 'Will I still get my expenses?'

'Oh yes. We're to go to my solicitor's office in the morning. He'll settle that side of things. I'll take you there.'

Amy came in having made coffee for all. 'Kind of an anticlimax, isn't it?' she remarked.

'Yes, I feel almost cheated,' Charlotte quipped. 'I was looking forward to doing my bit.'

Phil gave her a provocative smile. 'No reason why you shouldn't do your bit for me,' he said. 'Drink up, girls, and I'll take you both out to dinner to celebrate.'

'What about your wife . . . won't she be expecting you home?' Amy asked.

'Glenda isn't at home. She couldn't bear the suspense, so she's taken young Andy-Pandy over to Bristol to stay with her parents there. I said I might join her tomorrow night if all went well. But I don't have to, if you'd like me stick around, Carlotta.'

Charlotte gave him a remote smile. 'Do what you like, Phil, only don't count me in. I'll be going home tomorrow.'

Amy had been looking from one to the other with a degree of caution. 'Right,' she said, brightening, 'that seems all neat and tidy, and I don't have to act as referee, thank goodness. Well, if we're going out to eat, we'd better go . . .'

Phil walked them along to the little French bistro, which Charlotte thought was rather insensitive of him, considering he had as good as proposed to her the last time they were there. She doubted whether he even remembered that. Men were not the sentimental creatures women were, and tonight he was in jubilant mood, even ordering champagne.

She was wrong, though. When Amy left them alone for a few moments while she went to the cloakroom, Phil took Charlotte's hand and fondled it. 'Remember last time we were here?' he said, gazing deeply into her eyes.

She pulled her hand away. 'Yes, Phil. That seems centuries ago. I've done a lot of growing up since then.'

Phil sighed. 'You'll never know how much I missed you. You were not just an idle fling, you know . . . you meant a lot to me.'

He looked quite hurt when Charlotte laughed, but she couldn't help it. 'Sorry, Phil, but a good friend of mine warned me you'd say that.'

'Male or female?' he growled.

'Male, as it happens.'

'We-ell—there you go! I expect he was just afraid the old magic would get to work. And it has,' Phil went on moodily. 'Pity one can't have two wives in this country.'

Charlotte shook her head. 'Phil, you're hopeless! And I wouldn't be married to you for all the Crown Jewels. Your wife has my sympathy.'

'With girls like you around it's amazing how a defenceless man can stay faithful. But I am these days, honestly,' he said. 'Well, as good as.'

'I'm glad to hear it. Are you happy?'

He gave a roguish grin. 'Happier than I deserve, some people might say. How about you, Carlotta—anyone special in your life?'

'Mmm . . . not especially special but things are rather interesting at the moment. Which is why I'd like to get back as soon as possible.'

'I'm insanely jealous,' he sighed.

Amy coming back put paid to their exchange and they finished the meal over a general dissertation on people and times past.

'And do you mean to tell me,' Phil demanded, 'that you actually enjoy being buried down in the country? Cowpats on your doorstep and cocks crowing at dawn and all that?'

Charlotte laughed. 'We're not completely rusticated where I am. I mean, we have got running water and electricity. We've got the best of both worlds.' (Why did she have to say things that reminded her of Robert?)

'I should have thought you would have missed the high drama of hospital life.'

'Like a hole in head!' she scoffed. 'No more night duty or unsocial hours. It's great.'

'Listen, children,' Amy put in patiently, 'when you've finished discussing the fors and against, I'm on an early tomorrow. Can I please go home to bed?'

Phil signed the account and they walked back past brightly-lit shop windows to the quieter, darker side street.

Pausing when they came to the house, he snapped his fingers. 'Hell! Just remembered, I was supposed to ring Glenda. Oh well, a bit too late now. She'll probably be in bed.'

'Come up and try, if you want to,' Amy offered.

'Thanks, but I'd better not. I'll leave it till the morning. And where shall I meet you tomorrow, Carlotta? Holborn Station, nine forty-five? You're on the Central Line from here. It won't take you half an hour and it's only a short walk then to the solicitor's office.'

'Right, Phil. See you.'

He kissed her fondly goodbye. Then he kissed Amy too. 'Sorry to have barged in on your reunion.'

'Any time. Thanks for dinner.' She opened the door and the girls went into the house together. 'That wasn't too bad, was it?' Amy queried. 'I didn't quite know what to expect.'

Charlotte gave a relieved smile. 'No, amazingly once I got over the shock of seeing him, it didn't worry me. Must be hell to be married to, mustn't he? He ought to be fitted with a homing device.' They both giggled.

Up in the living-room they sat over a last drink, exchanging news.

'Sorry you got lumbered with my problems,' Charlotte apologised. 'How did Phil know I was going to be staying with you? I didn't tell him.'

'No, that was my fault. I met Anne Pointer at a party and we talked about it. She was the Sister on with you that night, wasn't she? And there were other people from St Chad's who were interested, so I suppose word got around. Lucky for Phil, the case being dropped like that. A pity it couldn't have happened earlier and saved you the trouble of coming, though.'

'Ye-es,' agreed Charlotte, 'but in a way it may have been for the best—my having to see him again, I mean. I'd been dreading it. And there wasn't any need. I'm fine,' she said happily.

'Why does he call you Carlotta?'

'It's Italian for Charlotte. His grandmother was

Italian.'

Amy smiled. 'Ah! So that's where he gets his dark good looks—*and* his penchant for the ladies. Look, you don't have to rush back to Yorkshire tomorrow, do you? Might as well make the most of it while you're here. We could do the shops in the afternoon and go on to a show in the evening.'

'I thought you were working?' Charlotte said.

'I'm on a half-day. I'll meet you back here after you've finished at the solicitor's.'

Charlotte went to bed and slept like a child, not at all bothered about seeing Phil again the next day. Her last thoughts were about the practice, and Niddborough, and how soon she could go back there without appearing ungrateful to Amy who had been really supportive.

Phil was already waiting at Holborn Station when Charlotte arrived the following morning. His arm went round her and there was no denying his welcoming embrace made her heart take a little leap. It was still exciting to be escorted by this loose-limbed, virile man, even though there was no more to it than that.

'Hallo, gorgeous,' he murmured, giving her a lingering kiss. 'Why was I ever crazy enough to let you out of my life?'

'You were probably very relieved when I faded quietly into the background,' she returned with a light laugh.

'Not true,' he declared, 'I had some bad moments thinking about us.'

'Well, all I can say is, good, because so did I for a

time. But not any more, Phil. The tide's gone out a long way since then, so let's just be friends, shall we?'

They began to walk towards the tree-shaded precincts of Lincoln's Inn Fields, beyond which the solicitor had his office in one of the ancient, time-honoured chambers.

'I'm forgiven then, am I? No hard feelings?' Phil pressed.

'You'll be asking for a medal next!'

He chuckled. 'Come back to London. If there weren't so many miles between us . . .'

Charlotte tutted and shook her head. 'So much for the reformation! Poor Glenda.'

'Poor Glenda, my foot. She does all right.' He paused outside one of the tall, mellow brick mansions bordered by neat iron railings, neat rows of small-paned windows gracing its classic lines and a well-polished brass nameplate by the front porch. 'Here we are, sweetheart.'

Phil took the four stone steps in a couple of long strides and pushed open the heavy oak door. A middle-aged secretary received them in the oak-panelled reception room and within a few minutes they were shown into the solicitor's book-lined office.

Mr Rubens had the appearance of a solid, upright citizen. Faultlessly dressed in a dark suit and crisp white shirt, he had a broad shiny forehead and the beginnings of a paunch. With due decorum he rose from his red leather armchair to shake them by the hand.

'Good morning, Dr Erskine and Miss Blythe—how d'you do? Please sit down.' He waved to a couple of chairs and smiled benignly at Charlotte when they were seated. 'Well now, we must apologise for your unnecessary journey, but we couldn't reach you in time to prevent it. I expect Dr Erskine has explained about the claimant withdrawing at the eleventh hour?'

Charlotte nodded. 'Yes, I'm really glad about that.'

The solicitor fiddled with his gold cufflinks. 'So are we all. Even though the facts were in our favour, you can never tell . . .'

They talked around various aspects of the matter, then Mr Rubens got down to the subject of Charlotte's expenses. 'Splendid,' he said having made a note of them. 'We'll get the account made out and you'll be receiving a cheque shortly. Will that suit you?'

'Yes, fine,' Charlotte agreed.

After a few more courtesies and a further shaking of hands, Mr Rubens wished her a good journey back to Yorkshire, then she and Phil were once more out in the pleasant morning sunshine.

'That was all satisfactory, wasn't it?' He took her hand and they made their way through the dappled shade of the green-lawned gardens. 'Coffee now?'

'Mmm—please. Then I'll have to get a move on.'

'Oh, don't go back today! I was hoping we could spend some time together.'

'Actually, I'm not going back till tomorrow,' she returned, 'but I have got plans for the rest of the day. Then I'll be off first thing in the morning. Sorry, Phil.'

'Oh!' he grunted. 'Can't wait to get back, it seems. What's this guy got that I haven't?'

Charlotte's laughter rang out. 'Does it have to be a guy?'

He stopped abruptly and turned her to face him,

searching her sparkling green eyes with critical candour. 'Yes, I'd say it does. Lucky devil. But I wish you joy, my sweet.' He bent to kiss her with some of his old ardour, crushing her body to his, the pressure of his mouth demanding.

She shut her eyes and tried to pretend it was Robert, but that was no use because the magic was missing. Not that she had much to make comparisons with—just that brief goodbye kiss at the station. And since that was about the only kind of kiss she was ever likely to get from Robert, it was pointless to fantasise.

All that was lost on Phil, however. He just realised he was getting no comeback.

'Come on,' Charlotte said, pulling away, 'or I shan't even have time for coffee.'

CHAPTER NINE

CHARLOTTE was light of heart as she stepped off the train at York that Saturday afternoon. Exactly why she felt in such good spirits she couldn't have said. True, it had been a tremendous relief with Phil's lawsuit being dropped like that; and also to discover that she no longer saw him through rose-tinted glasses. The skeleton in her cupboard had been brought out, dusted off and found to be just that—dry bones.

Her shopping trip and the West End show with Amy had been great, but she hadn't wanted to stay around for the rest of the weekend. She had made Lynne her excuse to hurry back, although Lynne had assured her she could manage.

What was so special about a small country town that made it seem like the most desirable place in the world to be in? she asked herself. All it represented was work —and Dr Challoner, of course.

Having to wait for her connection, it was another hour before she was back at the house in Spinney Lane. Lynne had arrived just a few minutes earlier, being driven back by her parents as Ken was on call that weekend.

Charlotte had already met Mr and Mrs Potter when she spent the weekend with Lynne at her home a couple of months earlier. They were a warm-hearted, friendly pair, greeting Charlotte like a second daughter and keen to hear all her news. A harmonious family atmosphere prevailed in the small living-room, adding to Charlotte's sense of well-being.

Mrs Potter made tea and produced a home-made Victoria sandwich. 'Now you're not slimming, are you?' she said, passing Charlotte a generous slice. 'It's been a waste of time making meals for Lynne this past week.'

Her daughter struck a model pose. 'Eight and a half stone, would you believe? Haven't I been good? I shall have to lay in a stock of willpower when I get back to work. It's going to be 'no' to all those home-made cookies I get offered.'

'And what do you think of this Ken of hers, lass?' Mr Potter asked Charlotte. 'All right, is he?'

'Yes, Ken's fine,' she returned with a sideways grin at Lynne. 'Not a breath of scandal, so far as I know.'

'Well, I'm glad she's got a sensible friend like you sharing the house with her,' Mrs Potter said, pouring more tea.

'Gee, thanks!' Charlotte laughed. 'My true worth appreciated at last.'

It was not until the parents had gone that the two girls could really get down to exchanging news.

Charlotte told Lynne about her Aunt Hannah's forthcoming appointment with Wendy Fenner, but Lynne saw nothing odd in that.

'I can understand it,' she said, 'especially if it's a very personal problem and their GP is a friend. After all, I wouldn't care to be intimately examined by any of the blokes we know.'

'Robert suggested she might be pregnant,' Charlotte mentioned.

'How come you were talking to him about it?'

'I wasn't directly, you know how these things just happen to crop up sometimes.' Charlotte eyed the telephone. 'I wondered if I ought to ring him? To tell him I'm back, I mean. Or would that look as if I were . . . running after him?'

Lynne found a knitting needle to scratch the inside of her plaster. 'Well, you do fancy him, don't you?'

'Oh God! It's not that obvious, is it?' wailed Charlotte.

'Only to me, don't worry. But if you feel like that, I shouldn't. If you think you should tell someone, ring Helen and let her know you'll be in on Monday.'

Charlotte acted on that advice and spent the rest of the weekend longing for Monday but determined to keep her wayward emotions well out of sight.

That Monday morning Robert was late in arriving at his surgery. Charlotte, after relating her story to the rest of the staff, was getting her treatment room ready for patients when he came to seek her out.

'Oh! So we've got you back, have we?' he said. 'Did all go well?'

'Yes, couldn't have been better.' She beamed at him and told him the details.

'I see.' He looked annoyed. 'Don't you think you might have found time to phone me? Or were you too busy celebrating with Superman?' he went on huffily.

'Well, we did celebrate, of course,' Charlotte admitted, 'but not just the two of us. I did think of calling you when I got back on Saturday, but Lynne came home that evening—her parents brought her—and we kind of got side-tracked.'

His long, invigilating scrutiny had the blood rushing to her cheeks and her heart banging against her ribs. 'And there was I worrying in case they'd locked you up!' he drawled.

'Gone are the days when I believed those sort of remarks,' Charlotte retorted perkily.

'Hmm! You seem to be your old chirpy self anyway, so I take it the bounce-back formula is still working?'

'Yes, I would say so.'

'You'll have to tell me the secret,' he growled. 'Tell me how I put it over to a mother whose son was the victim of a hit-and-run.'

So that was the reason for his short temper. 'Oh dear,' she said. 'Did he . . . die?'

'Yes. And I had to ask her for his spare parts . . .' Robert stalked through to his own surgery.

Gazing after him, Charlotte's eyes were wide with pity. She longed to give comfort but didn't know how. Poor Robert, sometimes it was too much to have to inflict more pain when there was already agony beyond bearing. But that was his role; he had to be strong for others, no matter how much it went against the grain.

If only she could just have held him in her arms! Biting her lip, she blinked back tears and wondered if he ever cried in private. Work intervened to claim her attention, but his troubled face continued to haunt her for the rest of the day.

He had gone on his afternoon rounds before Charlotte returned from lunch to deal with her afternoon baby clinic. That was the usual friendly, cheerful session, sharing with mothers the problems and progress of their infants. Giving one lovely baby boy his first protective cover against the scourges of whooping cough, diphtheria, tetanus and polio, Charlotte was reminded of little Baby Briggs. That poor little scrap with a runny nose and sore bottom and no one to love her, unlike this bonny lad.

Seeing the health visitor later that afternoon, Charlotte tackled her on the subject. 'Ruth . . . what happened about Baby Briggs—have you had time to follow that up yet?'

'Oh yes, love,' Ruth told her brightly, 'I reported about it on Friday, but of course you were away, weren't you?' She rolled her eyes. 'That was a cock-and-bull story the aunt told you. The mother's a nice kid and dotty about her baby, and her own mum's a perfectly nice woman, just a bit inadequate. They told me the aunt is jealous—can't have babies of her own and would like to take over this one. Apparently she offered to baby-mind and was just trying to stir up trouble.'

'Oh, so do you think things are all right there then?' Charlotte queried.

'Yes. They need a bit of help,' Ruth allowed. 'They're living in a couple of poky rooms—there's no husband around. I've put the social worker in touch to see if she can find them something better, and I'll keep an eye on them. They're scared of officialdom, but I'll try and get them to bring the baby to the clinic. Can't rush them, though.'

'Oh, thanks, Ruth,' smiled Charlotte, 'so long as I know you're keeping an eye on her.'

* * *

Charlotte's trip to London soon faded from her mind as she slotted back into her own busy world. All she had to remind her of it were some snazzy black tights and a stylish green sun-dress which she had bought on her shopping spree with Amy.

On Wednesday Lynne had her plaster removed and was thrilled to be free of it, making up for lost time by being able to use both hands at last.

'How does it feel?' Charlotte asked that evening, watching Lynne massaging Nivea cream into her dry, flaky hand and forearm.

'Terrific, really. I've got this brace I can put on for support if I need it, but a bit of physio and I'll be as good as new. Ken's coming round to take me out to celebrate tonight—just to the Cross Keys—want to come?'

'Not tonight, thanks all the same, Lynne. I've got a few things to do. There's my hair to wash,' Charlotte said, running her fingers through her tousled locks, 'and I thought I ought to tidy up a bit, in case Hannah wants to come back here for a cup of tea tomorrow.'

'Oh, for goodness' sake, I'll throw a duster around the place and put the cleaner over the carpet in the morning. Does she still bug you that much?'

Charlotte grinned. 'Not really. It's just that Hannah and tidying up go together in my mind. Anyway, you go, it's fine by me.'

She was upstairs in the bathroom with her head swathed in a towel when Ken arrived and Lynne called up to say goodbye. Hardly had they left the house when the telephone rang. Running downstairs to answer it, Charlotte felt her heart begin to pound when Robert's deep voice greeted her ears.

Since his frosty reception on her return from London they'd had little to say to each other, which had worried her. She wanted things to be as they were when he had seen her off from York. Warm and friendly, even if he was blind to the fact that she was hopelessly in love with him.

'Charlotte? Just checking the state of play,' he said. 'I've got a guilty conscience. If I snapped at you the other day, I'm sorry. You must think I'm an old grouch.'

She laughed softly. 'You were, but I knew you'd had a trying day . . . I can be magnanimous when it suits me.'

'All right, don't pile it on,' he protested, 'I still think you might have contacted me when you got back.'

'Sorry, Robert. I will next time.'

He grunted. 'Let's hope there's not a next time. Now, how busy are you?'

'Oh, desperately!' she joked. 'I'm not, actually. Why?'

'Could you be in a suitably baby-worshipping mood, then?'

'Yes, I could arrange that,' Charlotte said.

'Fine! I'll collect you in fifteen minutes and we'll go and brighten the lives of Mac and Naomi. All right?'

'Oh, great.' She spent the next fifteen minutes in a state of near panic, flying around getting herself ready. He must like her, musn't he? Maybe he was a little in love with her even if he didn't know it? But that was a dangerous pipedream when he'd already told her he had no intention of falling in love again. And how come she'd ended up apologising to him when he'd rung to apologise to her?

Pink-cheeked from hurrying, dressed in white trousers, a speedwell blue cotton top and her newly-washed hair shiny and fragrant, she was ready to leave when he called.

'Now that's what I call co-operation,' he approved, thinking how fresh and young she looked. In fact, utterly adorable.

'That's me,' quipped Charlotte, 'always prepared to be accommodating.' She picked up her shoulder-bag and they walked out to his car. 'Naomi's all right, isn't she?'

'Yes ... just a bit bored. We thought you'd be better company for her than Wendy.'

'Oh, discussed, was it?' She felt a little disappointed that she hadn't been a spontaneous choice on Robert's part.

He stroked his nose to smother a smile. 'Mac and I discuss many things, and not always to do with work. He's a great guy, is Mac. Behind that throwaway wisecracking he's sound as a bell.'

'I know,' Charlotte agreed, 'Naomi's one of the lucky ones.'

He gave her an odd sideways glance. 'Marriage is a two-way thing. It's finding the right match that's the problem. Something that's going to endure beyond that first excitement which knocks you for six.'

Sitting beside him she could feel the love welling within her. It was like a great tidal bore threatening to overwhelm her, and there was nothing she could do about it. She let out a long, tremulous breath and stared at the road ahead with unseeing eyes.

'What, no pearls of wisdom to amaze me?' he went on, with a satirical smile.

'If it's wisdom you want you should have brought Wendy,' she returned. 'I'm supposed to be light relief, remember?'

He laughed. 'You sound as if you're spoiling for a fight.'

'Of course I'm not. But I don't like being patronised.'

'And when Charlotte doesn't like, she has no hesitation in saying so,' he returned, his grin broadening.

'Would you like to turn around and take me home?' she snapped.

'No. For one thing we're nearly there, and for another they're expecting us, so you can cool it for a couple of hours. We can't disappoint them now.'

That was reasonable enough, so she gritted her teeth and kept quiet, and hated and loved him both at the same time.

The McAllisters lived in a pleasant newish bungalow on the outskirts of Ripley. Charlotte had never been there before, although she had met Naomi on a couple of occasions.

Naomi was a tall, well-built athletic girl who had taught games and PE at the local grammar school and was missing the companionship of those days. She was genuinely pleased to see her visitors. 'Charlotte—how nice of you to come,' she said. 'Don't you see enough of these men all day, without spending your evenings with them too?'

'That's true, but I've been longing to see your

baby,' Charlotte smiled, 'so I have to put up with the big boys as well.'

Mac kissed her exuberantly.'It comes to something when junior has more pulling power that his dad! Something I shall have to get used to, I'm afraid.'

Naomi took Charlotte up to the primrose-and-white nursery to see two-month-old Simon, sound asleep in his crib.

'Oh, he's gorgeous,' Charlotte breathed, gazing admiringly at the red-haired infant, long sandy lashes curling in half-moons on his plump cheeks.

'He's going to be the image of Gordon,' Naomi said with a fond smile. She sighed. 'I'll be glad when he's toddling, though. Babies at this age are so totally dependent, it's alarming. Do you think that sounds unnatural, Charlotte?' she queried, looking slightly anxious.

'Good heavens, no. It wouldn't do for us all to be alike, and with a first baby it's trial and error for everyone, isn't it? I guess I should be the same,' Charlotte went on. 'Anyway, you have got your tame expert on hand, haven't you?'

'You must be joking,' Naomi scoffed, 'he's more uptight about things than I am.'

Back downstairs in the living-room Mac produced coffee and hot sausage rolls and said how about a round of Bridge?

'Darling, you know I can't concentrate on anything like that at the moment,' his wife sighed.

'And Charlotte told me it was no good asking her to be intelligent tonight,' Robert said, a wicked glint in his eye.

'How about Rummy, then?' Charlotte suggested,

ignoring him, 'that won't tax anyone's brains too much.'

Mac produced playing cards and they settled down to the light-hearted pastime with a fair amount of barracking in between games.

'I saw a fan of yours at the hospital today Charlotte,' Mac said, dealing the cards once more.

'Not another one,' Robert put in. 'Who is it this time?'

'Terry Street—our resident bookie.'

'Oh! How is he?' Charlotte asked.

'Should be out sometime next week, all being well. And back in again if he doesn't do as he's told. His girlfriend has promised to see he cuts down on the booze and the fags.'

'What's the matter with him?' Naomi wanted to know.

'Got a heart problem,' Mac said.

'He's not the only one,' Robert muttered under his breath. 'Oh, I'm out!' He laid down his three kings and a run of four hearts, and scooped the kitty for the third time in succession.

'Your lucky night, Bob?' Mac grinned, stroking his sandy beard. 'Pity we're not playing strip poker.'

'Yes, that might have been interesting,' Robert agreed.

The girls exchanged tolerant glances.

'I should've thought you'd both seen enough naked flesh to last you a lifetime,' Naomi remarked.

A plaintive wail from the direction of the nursery interrupted further comments on that subject.

'Feeding time at the zoo. Go on, sweetheart, your son wants you,' Mac said.

She made a face at him and apologised to the others. 'Sorry to break up the party, folks, but that's life. Amuse yourselves for ten minutes.'

'May I come with you and pick him up?' Charlotte asked. 'I haven't had a cuddle yet.'

'Oh, sure.'

The two of them went upstairs and while Naomi got out a dry nappy and laid down a towel on the changing mat, Charlotte lifted up the protesting infant from his warm, cosy bed.

'There, there, sweetie,' she murmured, rocking him as he curled against her shoulder.

He gave an enormous belch, which had them both in giggles.

When he was once more clean and dry, Naomi sat down in her low nursing chair and undid her bra. 'Gordon says I shouldn't be embarrassed about feeding, but I'm damned if I'm going to whip my boobs out for a public peep-show,' she declared.

'No, I don't blame you.' Charlotte made herself busy straightening the cot. 'He's a really lovely baby though, Naomi. His grub must be suiting him. Do you feed on demand?'

'Open all hours? Blow that for a lark. The milk comes in at regular intervals anyway. I can plan my day better keeping to a timetable.'

Behind her pose of nonchalance, it was quite obvious that Naomi was loving every minute with her baby. This child was not likely to miss out on mother-love, Charlotte thought. She smiled. 'Well, I'll leave you to it, then. Are you going to bring him down when you've finished?'

'Oh, maybe just for a minute, but he usually falls

asleep halfway through his feed. Get Gordon to make some more coffee, will you please, Charlotte? We won't start playing again, will we?'

It was eleven when Charlotte and Robert took their leave of the McAllisters.

'Thanks for coming,' Mac boomed heartily.

'Yes, it was fun, wasn't it?' his wife agreed. She eyed Charlotte's slim hips. 'I must work on getting my figure back to reasonable proportions before you come again.'

'I love you just the way you are,' declared Mac, kissing her.

'Nice couple, aren't they?' Charlotte said, wistfully, as Robert's BMW sped through the dark lanes back towards the town.

During the evening her annoyance with him had disappeared, to be replaced by a desperate yearning for him to show her some sign of affection. She didn't care if he wasn't seeking a long-term relationship. It was now that was important. The future could look after itself. But when a look or a touch of his could turn her knees to water, how was she to bear it if he didn't want her?

'Yes, I knew you'd be good for her,' Robert said. 'You're good for me, too.'

'Why am I?' She stole a sideways glance at his strong profile, his expression thoughtful as he concentrated on the zig-zag descent down a steep hill.

They reached the bottom and he relaxed. 'Don't ask leading questions when I'm tackling difficult bits. Now, what did you say?'

'Why am I good for you?'

He half-grinned. 'Perhaps I should have said bad for me. Like alcohol.' He began to sing softly, *'You go to my head . . .'*

Charlotte laughed. 'If I didn't know you'd been on coffee all evening I should have thought you'd had one too many.'

'Do you mind if I stop the car? I can't concentrate on you and it at the same time.' He pulled off the road into a field entrance, switched off the engine and turned to look at her. 'Charlotte, Charlotte . . . you are just asking to be kissed, aren't you?'

'Am I?' she countered lightly, although her whole body tensed with excitement.

'Well, it would be a very pleasant way to end the evening, wouldn't it?' he murmured. 'Come here.'

In a moment she was where she longed to be—wrapped in his arms with his mouth finding hers. And his lips were persuasive and seeking, bringing her to heights of joy she could scarcely contain.

Briefly he pulled away, dropping butterfly kisses on her cheek, her throat, while he stroked the bare flesh beneath her cotton-knit top. Then he smiled roguishly. 'Necking in a car . . . juvenile, isn't it? I haven't done this for years.'

'Well, you don't appear to have lost your touch . . .' It seemed the most natural thing in the world to lift her mouth to his again and for a time there was silence while, finding her responsive, he made fiercely tender love to her.

For Charlotte time and place ceased to exist. She was lost in the utter bliss of his caresses. Her pulses clamoured for more. Her desire mounted, so that her body ached with wanting to give and give. And it was all so perfect, she felt it must be the same for him too.

It came as something as a shock when, quite abruptly, his embrace slackened and he took her hand from around his neck, placed a kiss on her palm and almost snapped, 'Right, little one, that's as far as we go. Time I took you home.'

She felt so humiliated she could have cried. It was like someone throwing cold water in her face. 'Fine,' she flared, shrugging. 'It was your idea to stop, not mine.'

Neither of them said any more until they reached Spinney Lane and he drew up outside the house. 'Goodnight,' she said primly, fumbling for the door-handle.

He caught her hand. 'Now don't go all sulky on me. You must admit things were getting rather too steamy back there. I don't want you to get hurt again.'

'Don't worry about me,' she said, 'I've got a hide like a rhinoceros now. I don't need anyone—least of all you.'

Dragging herself free, she ran up the path and let herself into the darkened house. It was a relief to find Lynne already in bed. She couldn't have faced having to explain the tears that were flooding down her cheeks.

CHAPTER TEN

SINCE her accident Lynne had got out of the habit of waking early. She yawned and stretched when Charlotte took her in a mug of coffee before leaving for work the following morning.

'Thanks, Lots,' she mumbled, only half awake. 'Where did you get to last night? Thought you were staying in?'

Charlotte perched on the side of the bed, sipping her own drink. 'An unexpected invitation. Robert took me round to see Mac's baby. Gorgeous little thing. He's got a mop of ginger hair, like his dad.'

Lynne opened both eyes a bit wider. 'And?' she said.

'And nothing. We played cards ... and then Robert brought me home.' She couldn't, just couldn't bring herself to tell Lynne what a fool she had been.

'Oh! Well, give it time, eh? He obviously likes your company.' Lynne heaved herself up the bed. 'By the way, did you see the note I left for you by the phone?'

Charlotte shook her head. 'No-I didn't go into the living-room.'

'Your dad rang. He'd like you to ring him back when you've got a moment. Nothing desperate, he said. Just something he wants to tell you.'

Charlotte glanced at her watch. 'Well, I haven't got time now. I'll do it in my lunchbreak. Don't forget, I may be bringing Hannah back after she's seen Wendy. It all depends what the problem is . . .'

'OK, OK, I'll tidy up. 'Bye.' Lynne turned over and went to sleep again and Charlotte went off to work.

It was the most beautiful morning, with the first flush of roses climbing rampant over cottage walls and a gauzy, fairytale mist lying across the river in the valley. But even with such a canvas spread before her Charlotte's spirits stayed at zero. Oh, stop being a twit, she reproached herself. Robert Challoner's not interested in you, and that's that. You'll get over it. You will. She knew it was going to be a hellish situation though, working together as they did.

Thursday was market day. Traffic was already building up around the narrow one-way streets leading to public car-parks. The congestion worsened when a small van in front of Charlotte blew a tyre and mounted the pavement. She got out of her car to see if anyone was hurt. Fortunately there were no casualties, but the passenger in the van greeted Charlotte like a long-lost friend.

'Hallo, Mrs Cooper,' Charlotte returned, recognising the battered face of the woman whose grazes she had treated the previous week. 'You all right, love?'

'Oh, just a bit shook up, Nurse.' Mrs Cooper patted the grubby dressing under her cheekbone. 'I kept the same plaster on this, like you said. I was on my way to see the doctor this morning . . . it's still very sore.'

'It would be. You had a nasty fall,' Charlotte

sympathised. 'Would you like a lift to the surgery?'

'That's right, you go with the lady, Ma,' her son put in. 'I'll be ages sorting out this lot.'

Charlotte arrived at work some fifteen minutes late.

'Robert was asking for you,' Helen warned. 'He seems to be in a right mood this morning.'

'Too bad,' Charlotte retorted. 'We got held up didn't we, Mrs Cooper? Her son blew a tyre, so I brought her in with me.'

She didn't hurry unduly. When she had taken off her jacket, and combed her hair, and put a few things out, she buzzed Robert over the intercom.

'Good morning. I believe you wanted me?' she said.

'Oh, Charlotte, yes. Just a urine specimen I'd like tested.' He paused. 'Are you all right?'

'Perfectly all right, thank you. A traffic problem this morning, that's all.'

'Right, come in, will you?'

With him in his office was a pretty, olive-skinned young woman with big dark eyes. He introduced her as Mrs Theophilou. 'It's a mild bladder infection,' he said, writing a prescription form and handing it to the patient. 'This should clear it up.' Turning to Charlotte, he went on, 'Get a mid-stream specimen, and if it's necessary we can send it away for analysis.'

Their eyes met and held. His were enquiring, hers deliberately neutral, although her limbs felt so unsteady she wondered they could support her. Turning away, she smiled at the patient. 'All right, Mrs Theophilou, if you'll come with me, it won't take a minute.'

The required specimen obtained and labelled, Charlotte chatted to the woman for a few moments. 'You and your husband run the Apollo Café in the High Street, don't you?'

'Yes, a year now since we opened, and business is good,' the woman said. 'You like Greek food?'

'Mmm, I'm very partial to a nice moussaka.'

'You come and see us,' Mrs Theophilou nodded, 'We give you a good meal,' she promised.

The morning passed slowly with mainly routine jobs that left Charlotte plenty of time for private reflection. And her thoughts were sobering. She must be a nutcase, allowing herself to fall for Robert, another of nature's charmers. As to having the hide like a rhino she'd boasted about, that was far from true. She was hurting so badly, the ache in her breast was a physical pain.

During her coffee break someone asked to see her in reception. She went out to find a smart young woman in black leather trousers and a belted primrose overshirt, clutching a bouquet of long-stemmed red roses. Thinking it must be a florist's delivery, for one heart-stopping moment Charlotte thought the flowers might be from Robert. The girl quickly shattered that illusion.

'Are you Charlotte? Here you are, love. Compliments from Terry. He's my chap—I'm Hilary—and he says I mustn't be jealous, because you saved his bacon.' She grinned. 'If I'd known what you were like, I might not have brought 'em.'

Charlotte laughed. 'I was only doing my job. Oh,

but these are lovely!' She admired the velvety blooms. 'Do thank him for me, won't you? Tell him they've really made my day.' They talked for a while about the bookmaker's progress, and the girl said they'd decided to get married when he came out of hospital.

Charlotte said she thought that was a great idea and wished them every happiness.

She put the roses in a vase on her desk in the treatment room, and every now and then she wondered just what the future might have in store for that couple.

Coming in to see her just before he was about to go on his rounds, Robert asked whether she'd done the urine test. A convenient pretext, she concluded. He was obviously worried about what had happened between them last night.

'Yes, NAD as far as I can see,' she told him, 'but I'll send it away to make sure.'

He nodded towards the flowers, frowning. 'Who are they from . . . Jack-the-lad?'

'From Mr Terry Street, actually.'

'Oh! Well, you're in no danger from him,' he said.

She carried on cleaning a dressings trolley, virtually ignoring him. 'I wasn't aware that I was in danger from anybody?'

He sat on the corner of her desk, watching her. 'Why are we so unapproachable this morning?'

'*We* are rather busy,' she said, wiping down the glass shelf with Hibisan, 'but if there's anything I can do, you have only to ask.'

He sighed, long and loud. 'All right, Charlotte, this isn't getting us anywhere. I'll see you later.' He strode away.

Charlotte washed her trembling hands and felt that she had come out of that encounter rather well. All the same, it was as much as she could do not to burst into tears.

At lunchtime she went out to do some essential shopping and brought sandwiches back with her to eat in the staff room. There was the ante-natal clinic later that afternoon, but the community midwife would be in attendance and Charlotte could have gone home for an hour had she not felt duty-bound to wait around for Hannah.

Thinking of family matters brought to mind the message to ring her father. She set about doing so and was lucky enough to catch him at hone.

'Dad? Lynne said you called me last night. Everything OK?'

'Yes, everything's well here, lass. How did your trip to London go?'

Charlotte laughed. 'Like a damp squib.' She filled him in on the details. 'I was going to try and come home this weekend, if that's all right?'

'Yes . . . I was hoping you could come fairly soon. There's someone I'd like you to meet.'

Charlotte's mind went back to her conversation with Woody, their daily help, and she smiled to herself.

'I see. What have you got to tell me, Dad?'

'Well, to get to the point,' he said, 'I've been seeing a lady, Charlotte, and I'm hoping to marry her. You wouldn't mind?'

'Mind? I couldn't be more pleased for you. Who is it? Anyone I know? Are you in love with her?'

Her father chuckled. 'Don't know about all that romantic nonsense. It isn't the same as when I courted your mother, but she's a good lass. We get on well. She was born into farming, so she knows what's what. It's Letty Rymer, from Kettleby . . .' He went on to remind her about the tractor accident when Farmer Rymer was killed.

Charlotte kept quiet about the fact that Mrs Woods had already primed her. 'Well, I'm thrilled to bits for you, Dad, I really am. And I'll look forward to meeting her. I'll be seeing Hannah this afternoon—does she know yet—is it all right to mention it?'

'Ah, Hannah.' Her father paused. 'Yes, you can mention it, although she'll not be pleased.'

'Whyever not?'

He sighed. 'It's a delicate subject. She stayed with us all those years, helping out. I know she had hopes, but I couldn't do it. It didn't seem right somehow, with her being your mother's sister. Anyway, she's got her own man now.'

Charlotte's brain was rapidly ticking over, working things out. 'Good heavens, Dad! It never ocurred to me she might fancy you . . .'

'Hush!' he said. 'Maybe I should have kept my mouth shut, but it might help to explain a few things. You were so much like your mother, I think she felt you stood in the way.'

It did indeed serve to explain a lot. As a child she hadn't realised what was going on, but now she could appreciate the bitterness of a disappointed woman. Charlotte hoped that nothing would emerge from her aunt's visit that afternoon to spoil her new-found happiness.

'Anyway, how is it you're seeing Hannah?' her father asked.

Charlotte remembered her promise to be discreet. 'She's shopping in Harrogate and said she might drop in on her way back.'

Shortly before two-thirty Hannah's dark blue Escort drove into the Health Centre car-park. Charlotte had been watching for her arrival and went out to meet her. They greeted each other with a peck on the cheek. Taking in her aunt's healthy colour, upright carriage and general air of well-being, Charlotte wondered if Robert's idea might be correct.

'Hallo, Hannah,' she said cheerfully. 'You're looking well.'

Her aunt made a dubious face. 'Looks can lie. I'm not right, or I shouldn't be here. There is a loo, I hope. I must go before I see the doctor. Is she here?'

'Oh, yes, there's her car.' Charlotte nodded towards Wendy's white Renault and led the way into the Health Centre. 'Come on, you can use the cloakroom next to my treatment room.'

When Hannah was ready they went along to Wendy's office where Charlotte made the introductions.

'Dr Fenner—this is Mrs Ormsby, my aunt.' Wendy rose to shake hands and they exchanged polite greetings.

'I'll leave you to it, then,' Charlotte said tactfully. 'I'll be in the treatment room when you need me.'

There was nothing for her to do as yet. She passed time going through stock, checking supplies, until Wendy sent for her some fifteen minutes later.

Her aunt was sitting by the doctor's desk, looking completely stunned. 'Y-you are—absolutely sure about this?' she pressed, picking nervously at her fingernails.

'Yes, Mrs Ormsby, absolutely,' Wendy said. She glanced at Charlotte with a detached smile. 'I've just given your aunt some startling news.'

Hannah turned a stupefied face to her niece 'I-I'm three months pregnant, she says.'

'Oh, Hannah!' Charlotte eyes shone. 'That's marvellous!'

'Well, I don't know . . .' Hannah's lips trembled. 'At my age? The baby could be—not quite right or something . . .'

Wendy, making notes, put her pen down and spoke firmly but kindly to the bewildered woman. 'Mrs Ormsby, I did explain how any abnormalities can be predicted at fifteen weeks, in which case something could be done about it. But women are giving birth much later in life these days, and there's no reason why you shouldn't have a lovely baby.'

'Oh God! Me with a baby? What will I do with it?' panicked Hannah.

Charlotte put an arm around her aunt's shoulders and gave her a squeeze. 'Just love it, and think how lucky you are. I know it's been a shock, but when you get used to the idea I'm sure you'll be walking on air.'

'Goodness knows what Oliver will say,' her aunt quavered.

'If I know men,' Wendy put in, 'he'll be tickled pink.'

'Do you really think so?' Gradually the beginnings of acceptance were taking root. 'Would you look after me? Take me through it?'

Wendy smiled but shook her head. 'I'm sorry, but I

may not be here much longer. I will recommend you to a good gynaecologist in your area, though. You'd prefer a woman?' Hannah nodded. Wendy looked up address, wrote a letter, sealed it in an envelope and handed it over. 'There you are, and the best of luck. Enjoy your baby.'

When they had parted from the doctor, Charlotte said, 'Did you really have no idea, Hannah?'

Her aunt shook her head. 'We-ell, I suppose it did cross my mind once, but it seemed highly unlikely at my age.'

'I think it's fantastic—a real bonus for you. I'd love to be a fly on the wall when you tell Oliver.'

'Yes, it is rather amazing when you come to think of it.' Hannah let slip a self-conscious smile.

Charlotte checked the time. 'I could take an hour off if you'd like to come back to my place for a cup of tea, to get your breath back?'

'No, I'd better go home and break the news. Anyway, thank you, Charlotte, for fixing the appointment. Just knowing I'm not ill makes me feel ten years younger.' They wandered out of the car-park. 'Where's Dr Fenner off to, then?'

'I don't know. That was the first I've heard of it,' Charlotte admitted. 'Now, you look after yourself, and if you ever want to have a chat about things, just call me. Love to Oliver, and give him my hearty congratulations.'

She waved her aunt off without having mentioned her father's wedding plans. She felt Hannah had had enough to cope with for one afternoon.

Going back into the centre, Charlotte made tea and took a cup in to Wendy.

'Did you mean that about not being here much longer?' she said, after they'd had a brief discussion about Hannah.

Wendy nodded. 'I really can't stomach all this baby business any more. It seems to come at me from all sides. Silly to let it bug me, I know. But it does. So I'm going into research with a pharmaceutical company. Mainly to do with haemophilia and other blood-related diseases. That way I shall at least feel less of a failure.'

'Oh, come on,' protested Charlotte, 'you're certainly not that. Far from it. Still, I know it must be difficult for you. We shall miss you,' she went on regretfully.

'Well, it's not common knowledge yet, but Dr Bates is going to come back for the time being, until they find another partner. I shall miss this place and everyone here. But I'm going to be much nearer London, which will suit me fine,' Wendy said cheerfully.

Outside in the reception area Helen was in a mild state of panic. 'I've just sent young Maureen home with a raging toothache,' she explained to Charlotte, clutching her brow. 'Mrs Clench has phoned to say she won't be in to clean in the morning as she's seeing the specialist about her haemorrhoids. And my husband has to rush up to Edinburgh tonight for a business meeting, so I simply must get away on time to make sure he's properly packed. He'd forget his head if it wasn't for me. Oh dear, it never rains but it pours, does it?'

'Well, that's all right,' Charlotte said, 'I'm in no hurry tonight. I'll stick around until the last patient's gone. You push off when you want to.'

'Oh, thanks, you're a pet. There'll only be Robert here for evening surgery. Wendy's finished after the ante-natal clinic, and Mac's on a half-day.'

Charlotte's inside flipped. She certainly didn't relish being in a one-to-one situation again with Robert after last night, but having offered, she could hardly back out now.

At five-thirty Robert returned to begin his evening appointments. Meantime Charlotte herself had a fairly brisk flow of people dropping in for advice, injections, blood pressure checks and so forth, so that she was surprised where the time had gone when Helen looked in to say she was leaving.

'There's just one more patient waiting to see Robert,' Helen said. 'I'll switch the phones over before I go.' She paused, lowering her voice confidentially and jerkng her head towards the waiting-room. 'It's that Mr Theophilou, from the Greek restaurant in town. He didn't have an appointment, but the doctor said it was all right for him to wait. Didn't his wife come in this morning?'

'Yes, that's right she did.'

'Well, he seems a bit agitated. I could imagine him turning nasty if he didn't get his own way. Still, I daresay Robert can handle him. He's a born diplomat. Must go. Goodnight, dear.'

There were no more patients for Charlotte either, and she employed the time tidying her treatment room while she waited for the doctor to finish. It had been a mentally exhausting day, what with her father's news, and Hannah's, and then Wendy's coming on top of her wretchedness over Robert.

She presumed Robert already knew about Wendy,

although he hadn't said anything. Robert the diplomat! Charlotte's lip curled. How dared he make love to her and then say he didn't want to hurt her? At least one thing was clear, last night had rattled him, even if he had started out with no more than a light flirtation in mind.

Picking up a pile of patients' records, Charlotte carried them through to the record shelves behind the reception desk. Slumped on a chair in the waiting area, the big black-haired man was rapidly licking through the pages of a magazine. When he glanced up, she smiled and said good evening.

He scowled back. 'How much longer must I wait?'

Fortunately, at that moment the doctor's office door opened, the previous patient came out and Robert himself appeared in the doorway. 'Mr Theophilou?' he said pleasantly.

Charlotte stayed to put away her records as the door closed on the two men. Then she went back to her own room, and pottered, keeping her eye on the doctor's surgery, intent on making a quick getaway when he had finished.

There was a frosted glass window between their two rooms through which she could see shapes and shadowy movements. With everyone gone from the Health Centre except the three of them, she could also here the rise and fall of their voices.

The dialogue rumbled on. It was easy to distinguish between the two men—Robert's voice moderate and controlled, and the patient's coming in excited bursts.

Charlotte frowned and leaned against her desk, watching the shadow play, feeling anxious. It was obvious there was some kind of argument going on in there which wasn't being easily resolved. In fact Mr Theophilou's attitude was getting more hostile by the minute.

At the Centre they were sometimes faced with awkward patients and it was policy to treat them with kid gloves, avoid confrontations if possible. Perhaps if she made an excuse to go in, a woman's presence might have a soothing influence . . .

As Mr Theophilou's voice grew louder her worry increased. Oh dear! It appeared that the man was accusing Robert of having an affair with his wife!

Robert's unheated courteous reply drifted through to her. 'My dear sir, I can assure you that my relationship with your wife is purely professional.'

'So what she come about, huh?'

'Just a simple health problem, which I'm afraid I can't discuss with you. But I've no doubt if you ask her she'll tell you about it herself. Now, is there anything I can do for you, Mr Theophilou?'

There was the sound of the chair being scraped back and the desk thumped with such vehemence that everything on it rattled.

'Liar! You make love to her, don't you?'

Hairs prickled the back of Charlotte's neck as further wild accusations were followed by the crash of breaking glass. She hesitated no longer. Outwardly calm, but inwardly quaking, she grabbed the first handy object—the sphygmomanometer in its oblong metal box—and marched in with it. She had no idea what she would find or what she could do.

She found the demented husband on his feet facing the doctor across the desk, a broken tumbler in one hand, his other raised menacingly. 'I teach you to leave my woman alone!' he roared.

Robert also was on his feet but showing no obvious sign of alarm as he considered the best strategy for dealing with this paranoia. To his dismay he saw Charlotte come in, walk straight over to the deranged Mr Theophilou and calmly take the broken glass from his trembling fingers.

'Oh dear, have you cut yourself?' she asked in a gentle voice. 'Sit down and let me see.'

At this unexpected intervention the man turned to her in a kind of stupor. His mouth gaped, then he dropped back on to his chair, buried his huge head in his hands and burst into convulsive tears.

Charlotte put her arms around his heaving shoulders, comforting him as though he were a child. 'There, there, it's all right, love. No harm done.'

'Sh-she was 'ere this morning, I know it,' he sobbed. 'She is so beautiful—no man can resist 'er. I love her so much—'ow can I not be jealous?'

Charlotte and Robert exchanged bemused glances as the sad story came spilling out. The Greek's wife had many lovers, he was convinced, although he could never prove it. He was sure it was the doctor this time, otherwise why did she come? She was not ill, was she?

'Just an infection, for which I prescribed some pills,' Robert told him kindly. 'Believe me, Mr Theophilou, your wife came to me for medical advice and that is what I gave. She's my patient. That was the only reason for her visit. You have nothing to worry about here.'

'And I was with the doctor when she came in this morning,' Charlotte affirmed. 'It was all perfectly correct.'

The man was clearly consumed with jealousy, whether with or without cause was not clear, but he certainly needed counselling.

After a little more straight talking, Robert said, 'If I make an appointment for you, will you go to see a friend of mine to talk about it? I think you'll find it would help.'

Mr Theophilou was finally persuaded. Charlotte poured him a glass of water and gave him a couple of Valium tablets to calm him down. He eventually left like a lamb, apologising for the trouble he had caused.

When at last they were alone Robert caught Charlotte by the arms and gave her a shake. 'What the hell do you think you were doing, tackling that maniac!' he yelled. 'God! He might have rammed the glass into your face. Then what should I have done?'

At first she laughed tremulously. 'Well, it worked, didn't it? He just fell apart . . .' Then, somehow, she was crying. 'A-all I could think of was what he might do to you . . .'

'Oh, my darling!' He gathered her close, stroking her hair and murmuring, 'My dearest love—if he'd so much as laid a finger on you, I should have throttled him.

They clung together in the discovery and joy of loving and being loved.

Finding no adequate words for what was in her heart, Charlotte lifted her tear-wet face to his, and their lips uniting told him all he wanted to know.

Presently, cupping her chin in his hand, he said, 'Do you think you could bear to be married to a secondhand old grouch like me? Because if you can't, I don't know what I shall do.'

With the fright of the last half-hour behind her, and glowing with happiness to find that he cared, her sense of humour bubbled to the fore. 'Whatever happened to the dedicated lone ranger?' she teased. 'Sure married life wouldn't get too steamy for you?'

He dug a finger into her ribs, making her wriggle and laugh. 'Listen, you!' he said, 'my willpower underwent a pretty tough test last night, and I flatter myself I came out of it rather well.'

'Apart from the fact that it completely demoralised me, you brute.'

'Now that's not a nice thing to call the man who's dying of love for you. I'm deeply hurt. Kiss me better.'

They both stopped clowning. Robert dispensed with anything at all resembling willpower and made her toes curl with delight.

'I love you, love you, love you,' Charlotte sighed. 'Is this really for real?'

'If that means yes, you'll take me on, it really is, my angel. You're not going to regret it, are you?'

'Robert, I was never more sure of anything in my whole life. I'm so happy, I could crow.'

He crushed her to him in a rapturous embrace. 'Then don't keep me waiting, sweetheart. I'll get a special licence, shall I?'

'Oh, can't I have a white wedding, and rice and confetti and all that stuff?'

Robert chuckled, a deep throaty, infectious sound which sent delicious shivers down her spine. 'My adorable, dotty, brave, silly, wonderful girl, you can have what you like so long as I'm included.'

Helen, coming back to the surgery at that moment, to make sure that all was well, saw the two of them clasped in each other's arms, oblivious of all else. She went quietly away again, a smile on her pleasant round face.

There had been speculation as to who would win the dashing Dr Challoner. So it was to be Charlotte, was it? Well, that was lovely. Helen could think of no better partner for him or for her. She had said all along they were meant for each other . . .

WORLDWIDE
MIDNIGHT STAR
She made him love her – that was her revenge